"Look, Brian," I said. "Accept some words of wisdom from Weatherby. There are a lot of us in this world who don't fit the mold—for better or for worse. Maybe we get some raw breaks, like our parents die, or maybe our parents are so screwed up themselves they don't even know we exist. That doesn't mean that something's wrong with us. It just means that we got some bad breaks. But sometimes that's good, because we have to make it by ourselves. And that makes us strong."

WEATHERBY

J.M.T. Miller

BALLANTINE BOOKS • NEW YORK

Library of Congress Catalog Card Number: 87-91471

ISBN 0-345-34464-2

Manufactured in the United States of America

First Edition: September 1987

CHAPTER
ONE

DESOLADO WAS A SLEEPY LITTLE TOWN WITH A POPU-
lation about the size of your average Saturday matinee
movie crowd. It was a two-hour drive southeast of the city
and the only watering hole for seventy miles in any direction. It was sun-baked, sun-bleached, and sun-drenched.
Even the saguaros looked thirsty.

I didn't have any trouble finding Sandy's Tavern. It was
in a bleak wooden building on the edge of the far side of
town. Stuck into the right front quarter of the building was
a small store. Its fly-specked window contained an age-
worn sign: FOOD, GAS & LIQUOR, ONE STOP. Above that
was a red and sky-blue neon beer sign.

A skinny old desert rat in denim coveralls was pumping
gas into a flatbed truck while the driver rearranged gunny-
sacks on the bed. The old man had a thin scraggle of yellow-gray hair atop his squarish head. His weathered face
lifted as I wheeled my ice-gray BMW into the gravel parking lot. He glared at me as I pulled up in front of the
tavern. I parked beside two hot-pink mopeds and a couple
of other cars.

Above the door, a rheumy neon sign blinked on and off,
almost invisible in the sunlight. I stepped inside and was
bathed in cool darkness. The smell of mildew, stale booze,

and even staler urine permeated the room. A country-and-western singer wailed on the jukebox, something about queers and beers and Texas and being lonely. Two worn pool tables with bare light bulbs hanging over them were wedged into the back of the room. Four pool racks decorated the walls. I stepped up to the bar and sat down.

The neon outside had lured in some of Desolado's downtrodden and hung over. Most of them were congregated at the far end of the bar, glued to a black-and-white television set, its sound competing with the jukebox for attention.

The woman behind the bar looked at me coolly for a moment before she swung her ample hips my way and muttered, "Yeah? What'll ya have?" She was massive and thick, and she came equipped with a triple chin. Her hair was piled up in a carefully lacquered crown of curls. She looked as if she'd slept in her makeup, then compounded the error by painting over it. She leaned closer and repeated, "What'll ya have?" Her massive breasts made giant, flat pancakes on the bartop.

"Orange juice, please," I said. "Fresh if you have it."

"Don't serve orange juice here, and I ain't got time for games. What'll it be?"

I hesitated, then said, "Maybe a bottle of mineral water? Flavored, please."

A scowl cut lines in the fat of her face. "This ain't no sody pop counter, buddy. You drinkin', er ain'tcha?"

I bowed to convention. "Uh—well, just gimme a shot and a beer."

That seemed to satisfy her. She turned to the tap. When the beer had foamed in the stein and she'd poured a shot of whiskey into a dingy glass, I decided it was time to pop the big question: "Pardon me, lady, but could you tell me where I might find a man named Tank Thaddeus?"

She stopped in mid-motion. her eyes did a rapid scan of my gray chinos and my white knit shirt—I got the feeling that I was dressed wrong—and then locked on to my face. She made a quick recovery, placed the shot and beer in front of me, and grunted, "Two an' a quarter, cash on the barrelhead."

I laid a five on the bar and said, "Tank Thaddeus? I'm sure you know him. He plays pool in here sometimes."

A veil dropped across her eyes. "Seems you know more about what goes on here than I do. I ain't never heard of him." She swooped the five off the bar, turned around, and hit a button on the cash register. With a little *ping* the drawer flew open. She slammed the five into the till, slid out my change, slammed the drawer shut, then turned and slapped the money onto the bar.

I pulled out my gray eel-skin wallet. She watched closely, her little eyes glittering with curiosity, contempt, and the first flickers of greed. I extracted a twenty, laid it on the bar in front of her, then reached inside my shirt pocket and took out a photograph. "Tank Thaddeus?" I said.

A man at the end of the bar had turned to watch us. "Hey, Mabel!" he called out. "Whensh Melvin comin' in? Don' know why you won' gimme a drink. He shesh he'll okay a tab for me anytime I want. . . ."

Her eyes stayed glued to the twenty. Out of the side of her mouth she said, "Can it, Mick. Why'ntcha get the hell outta here while ye're ahead? You still owe us fer the tab you ran last week."

"Ma'am," I said, "I assure you there won't be any problems if you tell me where to find Tank Thaddeus. I have an insurance check for him. He's most anxious to receive it. But I left the city without his address, and my secretary is out for the rest of the day."

She chewed on her lip. Her eyes narrowed. "Insurance, huh? Somethin' to do with that silver Harley he wrecked?"

"Sorry," I said. "That's confidential."

"Well. . ." She was still chewing on that lip.

The man she'd called Mick moved so fast I didn't even see him till he'd landed on the stool beside me. "You shay you're lookin' for Thaddeush?"

I nodded and pointed toward the picture. He said, "Cactush Corner Motel an' Geeradge. Last place on the corner, right beshide the shwimmin' pool.'' He stared hopefully at the twenty, while Mabel, hands on hips, looked as if someone had slid into her parking space.

I picked up the twenty and handed it to Mick. He folded it, stuffed it into a pocket of his baggy pants, then gazed wistfully at the shot and beer. I shoved them over to him. He grinned toothlessly, downed them both, then wheezed, ''Shay. Buy me 'nother drink an' I'll tell you where Thaddeush ish right thish minute.''

''You got it.'' Out came my wallet.

He grinned craftily and held out his hand. I laid a five in it. He cackled, then said, ''Shorta dumb, ain'tcha? Him an' that no-good gal of hish ish right next door—at old man Tucker's shtore.'' He belched softly, then hiccuped.

I was already up and moving out the door when I heard him wheedling. ''Shay, Mabel. No hard feelin's, huh? Gimme 'nother shot 'n' beer.''

CHAPTER
TWO

I WALKED OUT TO THE BMW, OPENED THE HOOD, AND pretended to examine the engine. I wanted a chance to observe my quarry when he came out of the store.

It worked. He clomped out the door, across the porch, and down the steps. The smell of stale sweat emanated from him as he passed by. His eyes flickered over me, then he gave my car a once-over. He stopped beside one of the hot-pink mopeds, his face wrinkled into a frown as he stared into the distance.

It was Tank Thaddeus, all right.

He was heavy leather and axle grease, with thick reddish brown hair that had overgrown his ears and neck and partly obscured his shoulders. Thick tufts of hair sprouted from his collarbone. The three skull-and-crossbone rings on his right hand were as good as conventional brass knuckles, and twice as legal. They gleamed evilly in the late-afternoon sun. His dirty, broken nails were ridged with grease. He wore heavy boots and tattered Levis held up by a length of chain. A leather vest partly covered his muscle-swollen chest. His biceps were the size of my thighs.

He stared at the sagebrush–dotted landscape, scratched his bearded chin, then swung astride one of the mopeds.

Looking like a gorilla on a tricycle, he kicked the starter. The machine sputtered, then died.

I closed the hood of the BMW and stepped over to him. "Pardon me. Can I talk to you for a moment?'

He looked at me with deep-set olive-green eyes and groaned "Hunnnh?" His voice resembled a dump truck unloading gravel.

"Are you Tank Thaddeus?"

His head tilted. He frowned, his heavy, dark red eyebrows sliding down to half cover eyes in the process of switching from empty to suspicious to angry.

I tried again. "Are you Mr. Thaddeus?"

The cogs and wheels were turning slowly. Finally he said, "Uh—so—who wants to know?"

"Me."

"You—uh—you somebody?" He scratched again at his ragged beard. He looked genuinely bewildered.

"I'm Weatherby. Artie Weatherby. Are you Tank Thaddeus?"

"Uh—who wants to know?"

Apparently, he didn't comprehend. I said, "Me. Artie Weatherby."

"Don't know you," he said with uncertainty. One heavy boot hit the kick starter again. Again, the engine sputtered. He cursed, kicked again, and it came to life with a ladylike cough. He turned his head toward the store and shouted, "C'mon, Bunny!"

A tall, thin blonde in cutoff Levi's came through the screen door. It banged shut behind her. She was carrying a large paper bag of groceries. The white of her enormous breasts peeked out over the top of a red tank top. She was a little thin in the legs, a little angular, but she'd do. She'd definitely do.

"Bay-bee!" Her husky voice punctured my fantasy. It was a whine that approached aggravated assault. "When you gettin' your Harley fixed, Bay-bee? I hate—ha-ate!—these damned toys." She tied her grocery sack on the back of the second moped and climbed astride.

"Shaddap, Bunny." Tank's voice was flat.

I raised my voice above the putting of the moped. "Mr. Thaddeus, your sister Jill sent me."

Bunny's head jerked around at that. She looked at me with hard, pale little eyes that were set close together, then she turned quickly to Tank. For an instant I thought I saw a dim fear trickle through Tank's flat green eyes, then he said, "Uh—look, mister, I don't know who you are—"

"Weatherby. Artie Weatherby."

"—but I don't want nothin' to do with my, uh, my sister. Tell her I don't want nothin' to do with her scheme. That—uh—that I ain't coming back to the city. Tell her that that bigshot boyfriend of hers is—"

"Tank!" Bunny said sharply. "Let's get the hell outta here!"

Tank's face crumpled, and for a second I thought he was going to cry. Instead, he threw back his head and started laughing. He sounded like a deranged seal.

"Laugh, you asshole," Bunny snarled. "If I so much as told Nails that you were talking to *anyone*—"

His head swung slowly around and he stared at her. She shut up.

He gave her a quick nod and she kicked her moped into life. In a flash they were flying down the highway into the desert.

CHAPTER
THREE

BEHIND ME, THE SCREEN DOOR BANGED. I TURNED
around. It was the old man who'd been pumping gas.

"Ain't no good." Having made this pronouncement, he
spat into the dust beside the porch railing.

"True," said I. "People like that are a blight on the
neighborhood."

"Not them," he groused. "I mean these here durn pistachio nuts. Ain't no durned good. Too much salt. Salt's
hard on the heart, sonny. Got to worry 'bout things like
that when you git to be my age." He spat again, then
looked at my car with resentment. "You young punks don't
know when you got it good. That yer car?" He pointed.

I nodded.

"Stolen?"

I let it slide. "Do you know the man who just left? Tank
Thaddeus?"

He squinted suspiciously at me and said, "Can't say as
I do. You want to buy somethin'? Gas? Beer?"

"No, I just need to know if you know Tank Thaddeus."

"You tryin' to start some durn trouble, young fella?
'Cause if you are, ain't no trouble a'tall to call old Bryce
Canyon. He's the law around here."

I bowed to the inevitable. I opened the old gray eel-skin

and extracted a twenty. Someday I'm going to write a book called *One Thousand and One Ways to Extort a Private Eye*. I folded the twenty in half, handed it over, and asked again, "Tank Thaddeus?"

The bill vanished into the pocket of his overalls and he was suddenly friendly. "You mean that biker just left here? One you was yellin' at?"

"I wan't yelling."

He chuckled. "Thought fer a minute you was after that durn gal."

The gleam in his eye turned raunchy. "That gal sure is somethin'. Loves to jiggle them big jugs at anybody'll take the time to look."

I let that slide, too. "What do you know about Tank Thaddeus?"

"Can't say as I know much a'tall."

I held my hand out, palm up, and nodded toward the pocket into which the twenty had vanished.

"But I'll be durned pleased to tell you what little I can," he said.

"Do you know him personally? Talk to him?"

His eyes turned crafty and he scratched at a thin stubble of hair on his square chin. "Can't say as I do. That gal, now—she's somethin' else. . . ."

"How long has Tank been down here?"

"Ain't been here so long as the rest of them bikers. 'Spect the first time I seen him was about a month er so ago. Come ridin' in on that silver Harley of his with that gal behind him, bought a quart of Jim Beam and a six-pack of Coke—er, I mean Sprite."

"Do you know anyone named Nails?"

The question surprised him. "Nails? Why, shore, sonny, he's that gal named Bunny's brother. President of the Satan's Sadists. Owns the Cactus Corners Garage and Motel. That's why them bikers headquarter out there now—that and other things." He was enjoying his erudition. He gave me a crafty wink. "You heard tell of Satan's Sadists, ain't you, sonny?"

"No," I lied.

"Well, you go ta messin' with Thaddeus or Nails, and you will hear about 'em, sonny, you durned well will." He cackled with relish at the thought, then confided, "Them boys will stop at nothin'. Why, they—"

"They what?"

"Say, sonny, I don't know who you are, but I ain't gettin' myself mixed up in this fer no twenty dollars. No sir, old Uriah Tucker's price is a little higher these days." As if envisioning a future too golden for words, he looked into the sky beyond me and said, "Why, in no time a'tall, I'll be lightin' my cee-gars with twenty-dollar bills—" Again suspicious, he grunted, "Say, sonny, who are you?"

"My name is Artie Weatherby."

"Nyuk," he snorted. "Nyuk, nyuk. Dumbest durn name I ever did hear. Ain't a name that cuts no cake 'round here anyways."

I could see that it was time to pull rank. I flipped open the eel-skin and showed him the photostat of my P.I. license.

He squinted at it, rubbed his eyes, and said, "So you got a durn piece o' paper with squiggly chicken tracks on it. So what?"

"You got glasses?" I asked.

"Don't need 'em."

I bowed to the impossible and put my wallet away. "Look, I need to talk to Thaddeus. Can you call him, tell him I need to see him? It's important."

"I got problems, you got problems, we all got problems," he said. He swiped at his forehead and said, "Too dratted hot out here today, if you ask me. Be movin' to the city soon. Have me a fine place to live. . . ."

"Are you inheriting some money?"

He snickered. "Ye're a funny feller, sonny. Guess you might say I am at that. Say, don't get much company out here these days. How's about a beer? A beer an' some pistachios. Just opened me up a bag of pistachios. You like 'em?" He looked at me hopefully.

I looked at my watch. Five o'clock. "Thanks," I said, "but I'll have to pass." I took a business card out of my card holder, wrote across the back, "Tank, call me. Urgent!" then handed it to Tucker. "I wonder if you'd be kind enough to give this to Thaddeus the next time he comes in the store."

He held the card at arm's length, then said, "What is it, raffle ticket er somethin'?"

"My address and phone number," I said. "And if Tank gets the message, I'll see that you get another twenty smackers."

He gave me a yellow-toothed grin. "Long as it don't cost me nothin', don't see why not. Nosirree, sonny, don't see why not. Sure you wouldn't change your mind about a pistachio? Hate to waste 'em.

"No, thanks," I said. "I have to get back to the city."

CHAPTER
FOUR

As I DROVE NORTH, THE SKY BECAME A PASTEL WATER-
color above the pewter bay. The freeways shone like luminous gems. The skyscrapers downtown were spills of
light against the darkening backdrop of sky and water. Dusk
was transforming the city into soft lights and glitter; night
would transform it again—into gaudy neon and black al-
leys, into something hard and gritty and violent.

I stopped at a Quickway for a crisp head of lettuce, some
tomatoes, a cucumber, a pound of liver, and a loaf of rye
bread. I made a second stop at the Whole Earth Health
Food Store and bought two six-packs of lime-flavored mineral water.

The sky was inky by the time I turned off El Agua Drive
and onto Sherwood Road. The drapes in picture windows
were open, revealing little pastiches of family life. Sprink-
lers watered lawns; children played in lighted backyards.
Here and there the aqua blue of a well-lit pool illuminated
the night. A couple of families were having barbecues.

I drove beyond it all, up through the canyon and to my
rented bungalow. It stood there, isolated and stately against
the dark cut of the canyon with its cover of ironwood,
scrub oak, and eucalyptus.

I carried the groceries into the kitchen, flipping on lights to drive out the ghosts. I showered and put on a pair of white denim shorts. Then I went back into the kitchen, put the liver on to fry, and made myself a huge salad.

When it was time to turn the liver over, I sliced some sweet onions into the pan, then stuck two slices of rye bread into the toaster. When they popped up, I spread them both thick with hot mustard.

The liver and onions browned perfectly. I forked the liver onto the toasted bread, covered it over with the sauteed onions, then pressed another slice of toast atop it. I put the skillet under the faucet, filled it with water, and left it there to soak.

My clock said five till eight. I arranged the sandwich and salad on an antique silver tray, added a large glass of milk, then carried it all into my small living room. I placed the tray on the Mexican mosaic coffee table, sat down on the sofa, picked up my remote control, and turned on the television.

My favorite show had just started. It was on UGTV, a new underground cable station that specialized in weird programming. The show, usually broadcast live, had been on the air for about six months.

The theme played, a Muzaked version of Steppenwolf's "The Pusher," an oldie and goldie like Bert Baxter, the host. Baxter had been around longer than I could remember, but he still maintained a certain cap-toothed tuxedoed elegance. I have to admit I liked the guy. He stepped forward and oozed some charm. The music faded, and he said, "Good evening, ladies and gentlemen. Welcome to the *All-New What's My Line?*"

Whistling and canned applause erupted from the non-existent audience. The camera moved in for a close-up of Baxter, then he said, "Today our show is brought to you by Pink Heart Pharmaceutical *and* our very own Green Mountain Ambulance and Mortuary!" He flashed rows of capped teeth and dimpled into the camera. "We'll be *right* back. But first, this word from our sponsors—"

A commercial flashed on the screen. I bit into my sandwich as a pompous, silver-haired pitchman began expounding on why I should let him bury me. I switched channels.

John Wayne was herding cattle across the Red River for the nine-millionth time. I switched channels. Some Japanese man was about to stick a sword into a kimonoed woman. She fluttered her eyelids and burst into song. I switched channels. Bert Baxter's smiling face was back on the tube.

"And now for our show!" he said, then waited for the canned applause to subside. "First, let's meet the panelists!" More applause. "Our first judge tonight is Grady Murphy!"

The camera zoomed in on a man in his late fifties with a raw face, a steel-gray flattop, and bloodshot eyes. Baxter's voice continued: "Mr. Murphy is a police officer from the Bronx, New York! Aren't we *luck-ee* to have such a well-qualified judge on our show tonight?" The tape-recorded audience roared their agreement. I swallowed my last sip of milk.

Baxter held up his manicured hand. The applause faded as if he'd gestured to real people. I took a bite of salad.

"Our next judge is Mildred Sweeney, a nurse from Topeka, Kansas!" Again there was applause as the camera closed in on a thin, birdlike woman with frizzy hair and granny glasses. "And our third and final judge is a special treat, ladies and gentlemen—a man who was recently placed on parole after serving eight at Leavenworth for heroin trafficking! Ladies and gentlemen, meet Mr. Pacman Jackson!"

Thunderous applause accompanied this introduction. The camera zeroed in on a huge black man with a wide, leonine nose, a short Afro, and a grin that was all razor blades and glass. He said, "Pleased to be out amongst ya all again, blood!" The applause machine went crazy.

When the din subsided, Baxter turned to the three panelists all of whom perched behind miniature judges' benches, and said, "Now let's ask our beautiful Roving Retrievers, Betty and Veronica, to bring in . . . *our first contestant*"

The theme song played again, an up-tempo version with

a reggae beat. Two voluptuous amazons came forward. They both wore French-cut briefs, black net stockings, and high-high-heeled shoes. They also wore white ward attendants' jackets. Between them was a kid of about nineteen dressed in grimy Levi's and a rag that had once been a tank top. He had acne, a surly expression on his face, and glazed eyes.

The two amazons escorted the boy to a chair in front of the judges' podiums, then stood at full attention on either side of him.

"And now, judges," Baxter said, "here's your report on the contestant. Betty and Veronica found him in a bar called the Gin Mill, on Juniper Road. Sorry"—he flashed his teeth and dimples at the same time—"that's all the information I'm allowed to give you. And now, the clock is ticking."

The theme music was playing again, this time with heavy clock ticks as a background beat. Then Baxter said, "Judges, you all know the rules. You'll each have one minute to question our contestant. You must try to answer his big, *bi-ig* question: *What's My Line?*"

I chewed on a bite of salad, studying the kid closely. I decided he was on Quaaludes and crack. They never get strung out on just one thing anymore.

"Young man," asked the nurse primly, "do you live in the area where you were picked up, or were you just visiting?"

The boy snarled an obscenity at her and flipped her the bird.

"Oh, my goodness!" Nurse Sweeney exclaimed. Then she tried again. "Young man, when you're high, do you hallucinate?"

He flipped her the bird again and added, "Screw off, grandma."

She said, "Well, I never. Try to help someone out—" Just then my phone rang.

I turned the volume down and picked up the phone. "Yeah?" I said. "Make it snappy."

"Mr. Weatherby?" a woman's breathy voice inquired.

It was the same voice I'd first heard three days ago, the one with the finishing-school diction.

"Yeah?"

"It's me, Jill Thaddeus. When I first phoned and asked you to find my brother, I couldn't meet you because I had to go out of town. Well—uh—my trip was canceled at the last minute. I've been trying to reach you all day. I need to see you, Mr. Weatherby."

"I'd planned to call you tomorrow," I said shortly. "I've already found your brother."

"What—what was he doing?"

What was he *doing*? Not *where was he*, but what was he *doing*? I didn't like that. I replied, "He was cruising around in the desert on a pink moped."

"Oh, no." With a little intake of breath, she said softly, "Then he's still alive?"

I didn't like that either. "He's still alive. Is there some reason he shouldn't be? Look, Miss Thaddeus, I told you three days ago it was against my better judgment to accept a case over the telephone. You assured me that it was a simple matter of your brother's leaving home after getting mad at you and your father. Nothing complicated. When your chauffeur arrived with your brother's photograph and the retainer and the letter of authorization, I figured you were on the up-and-up."

"Oh," she said. "I was. I—I *am*."

"Maybe you'd care to explain why you sounded so disappointed to learn he *was* still alive."

"Oh, no!" She sounded horrified. "It wasn't that. It's just the moped. Pink, you say?"

"Yeah. Just like a baby's booties."

"Oh, no," she repeated. "Look, Mr. Weatherby, I need to see you right away. I'm grateful to you for finding my brother, but some other things have come up. Could you meet me right away?"

I looked at the television set, then looked even longer at my bed. But I said, "All right. Give me an hour. Where do you want to meet?"

She hesitated, then said, "We have to be discreet, you know."

"Why?"

"I'm—I'm engaged.

I didn't bother to hide my irritation. "How about a nice little out-of-the-way motel I know over by the railroad tracks? Adult movies? No one would ever find out about our rendezvous over there. We can even pay by the hour."

Evidently the sarcasm went right past her, because with the same innocent tone, she said, "No, that wouldn't do. It's too far away. I can only be gone for an hour or so. Couldn't we make it closer? Maybe somewhere halfway between your place and my father's estate in Brevity Hills?"

"Ah, hell," I said. "Look, do you know La Fiesta? The Mexican restaurant and nightclub over on Hathaway and Vine? Meet me there at ten."

"That will be fine. But how will I recognize you?"

"I'll be wearing a black mask and holding a rose in my teeth."

"Won't that attract a lot of attention?"

She was related to Tank Thaddeus, all right. "Seriously," I said, "I'll wear charcoal slacks and a white shirt, maybe my gray suede jacket. I'm six foot one and I have dark blond hair. I'll be there at ten. Anything else?"

"I'm at my father's now, so I can't change," she said. "I'm wearing a beige dress, a red jacket, and I have dark auburn hair, shoulder-length."

"Great," I said. "Anything else? Because I'm still in a hurry."

She hesitated, then finally replied, "I guess not. It can wait."

"Good. Thanks for calling." I hung up.

I hit the audio on the set just in time to hear Baxter say, "And now, in answer to all your guesses, our contestant will answer the big, *bi-ig* question: *What's My Line?*"

The young man stood as the camera moved in closer to him, heightening the suspense. He snarled, then mumbled something into a mike that one of the amazons had thrust into his face.

"What?" Baxter said. "What's that? Speak up, please."

Baxter leaned in to hear the reply, then turned to the camera, flashing his million-dollar smile. "And thaaat's it, folks! Our medical advisor has already run the blood tests that confirm what our young guest has just told us. Our contestant's li-ine is . . . *wine!*"

The phantom audience roared and whistled again.

The Bronx policeman looked fatalistic. Nurse Sweeney appeared to be having a heart attack. The black dealer looked ecstatic. He muttered, "Wine, man. I knowed it was wine!"

The nurse began whining. "I tell you, that wasn't a bit fair. It was supposed to be drugs, not alcohol—"

"Lady," the cop interrupted her, "alcohol *is* a drug. You should know that."

"The Pusher" was playing again as I switched off the TV. I took my dishes into the kitchen, rinsed them off, then stacked them in the dishwasher. Back to the real world.

There was something about Miss Jill Thaddeus' attitude that rankled, something about her stories that wasn't matching up, something about this whole deal I didn't like. But I did like her five-thousand-dollar retainer.

I brushed my teeth, then was on my way.

CHAPTER
FIVE

LA FIESTA'S LOUNGE WAS DIM AND MISTY WITH SMOKE. Barely visible on the white stucco walls were huge murals made from shards of broken glass and illuminated softly from behind: a charging bull, a gored matador, a rose with blood drops seeping from it.

Jill Thaddeus was drinking her margarita from a long-stemmed crystal goblet. Mine sat in front of me, untouched. A combo made up of a piano, a guitar, and two violins was playing something sad and Spanish.

The mosaic-topped cocktail table was low, the chairs even lower. Jill turned slightly and crossed one long, lovely leg over the other. She's had a lot of practice at getting the hemline to fall just right—halfway up her thigh. Nice effect, even if studied. Sheer stockings above satin beige pumps. A flash of sleek thigh, a little tug of the hemline to emphasize the routine and confirm that it was strictly for show. She bit her lower lip, then looked across at me. "Tank actually said he wants nothing to do with me?"

"That's what he said. Nothing to do with your *scheme* or your *big-shot boyfriend*. The words are his, not mine."

She turned a shade paler. Even in the dim light it was apparent. "He actually mentioned my—my boyfriend?" she asked softly.

"That he did."

"But what are they *doing* out there?"

"Sorry. The assignment was to find him, not investigate what he was doing."

"Could you find out?"

"I might be able to. It would depend."

She took a tiny sip of her drink, a small, pink tongue darting out to lick the salt from the rim of the glass. She swallowed, then said, "You see, Mr. Weatherby, my brother—he's never been—well, I guess *normal* is the word. He seems to get worse every year. I'm worried about him. Deeply worried."

"Any special reason?"

"Ever since he got involved with that motorcycle club— the one with the awful name—he's been getting stranger."

"Think it might be drugs?"

"Oh, Mr. Weatherby, it could be, couldn't it? I'm so worried. Couldn't you *do* something? Make him come home?"

"I'm not the Gestapo, lady. Just a private eye. I can't force him to do anything he doesn't want, unless I kidnap him and hold him prisoner. If you need that sort of work done, you want to hire the Mafia."

She paused, sipped her drink again, then seemed to make up her mind about something. She pursed her lips as if she had something distasteful to reveal. "Mr. Weatherby, my brother's real name is Abernathy Thaddeus the Third. Does that ring a bell?"

"It jarred my socks a little, but I didn't hear any bells."

"Excuse me?"

"I said no."

"Oh. Well, my father is Abernathy Thaddeus the Second, the philanthropist. The pet food heir? Surely you've heard of him."

"I seem to remember something about his endowing the zoo with three million dollars or so."

"That's him. But he hasn't turned the money over yet. The endowment is still in the talking stage. And the zoo isn't going to get that money if I can help it. That's why I needed to see you. My father is old—eighty-one—and an unusual man. This thing with Tank has been hard on him.''

"Well, your brother is alive," I said. "That should be good news to your father." I leaned back in my chair and crossed my legs. My kneecaps stuck up between us. I uncrossed them.

She waved a hand adorned with a three-carat, emerald-cut diamond engagement ring and said, "Actually, my father's dilemma is far more pressing right now than figuring out what Tank is up to.''

"What dilemma is that?" I asked.

"Oh, you'll want more money, of course. I've been told you don't come cheap.''

I sat forward. "My terms of employment with you have been fulfilled. If something else is required, I'll have to know precisely what it is before I decide whether or not I'll take the job.''

She fluttered her hand back and forth. "It doesn't matter. I have enough money. At least, I do right now.''

Flatly, I said, "Lady, some jobs I do; some I don't. Let's hear what you want, and *then—if* I take the job—we'll talk about money.''

She leaned her elbow on her knee, bent her head, and tilted her chin into her cupped hand. Then she lowered her eyes slowly, to look at the floor. As if to herself, she said in a hurt little voice, "I suppose I'll just have to put up with being treated like this.''

Drama! I waited.

She looked up at me, her eyes wide and innocent. "Tell me, Mr. Weatherby, do you believe in werewolves?''

"What?"

She smiled faintly, embarrassed, and sat up straight again. "Werewolves. Do you believe in them?''

"You've got to be kidding." I was beginning to get a feeling about the Thaddeus family. They all belonged in a box of Cracker Jacks.

"Mr. Weatherby, I'm serious. *Do* you believe in were-wolves?''

"Just werewolves? Not vampires or ghouls or ghosties?

How about things that go bump in the night? I believe in them. I did that a few times myself, before I gave up the juice.''

"Juice?"

"Forget it!"

Her olive-green eyes grew rounder. "You mean you won't take the job?"

"No, I mean forget about the juice."

"Then you will take the job?"

I returned her gaze, not saying a word, but she knew what I was thinking, because she said hastily, "The problem is my father."

I nodded and said, "Now we may be getting somewhere. I wouldn't know yet."

She fluttered her hands and turned her head delicately to another equally flattering angle. "Mr. Weatherby," she began with a lowered voice, "please excuse me. I—I've led a rather sheltered life. I haven't had to mix much with the well, the common people. I've never met a private investigator before."

She waited to see if her little speech had touched my heart. I waited, too. She sighed, wistfully. I waited.

"Mr. Weatherby," she said at last, "I haven't been able to live at home for five years. My father is too difficult. The only person able to influence him is his housekeeper, Miss Partridge. She's been with him for twenty years, and he seems to do almost everything she tells him to. She's poisoning him against Tank and me, slowly getting him to believe that we're spoiled, ungrateful brats. He's already cut Tank off from the family money, and he's talking of doing the same to me if I go ahead and marry my fiancé."

"So he plans to leave the family fortune to his live-in housekeeper?"

Her eyes went wide again. "You don't understand. You see, my father—uh—well—he likes animals."

That embarrassed me. I said, "Well, there are a lot of good therapists in the city. . . ."

She shot me an angry look. "I don't mean *that* way. I mean—well—he has bats in his attic."

"Don't you mean bats in his belfry?"

"No, I mean bats in his attic—oh, never mind! No one ever believes me. You'll see."

"I'll see what?"

"What I mean."

"Someday maybe. In the meantime, I think I'll go home and sleep on it." I stood up.

"Mr. Weatherby?" Something in her voice caught at me. It was the first real emotion I'd detected from her. I sat back down.

She was twisting her hands together, tearing at her engagement ring. Her voice was shaky as she continued. "Mr. Weatherby, my father thinks he's turning into a werewolf."

"A *what*?"

The tears were real, and they were rolling down her cheeks. She looked into my eyes, her own full of misery, and said, "My family is cursed."

I just sat there.

She stifled a little sob. "Oh, I knew you wouldn't believe me. Worth doesn't believe me either."

"Worth?"

"Dr. Worthington Sterling, my fiancé. He just tells me not to worry, that things will work out. He actually went out to the house when I first met him and—and took *pictures* of Father! He told me that he'd prove Father wasn't turning into anything but a nasty, greedy old man. I can't get Father to see any doctors, and every day he gets worse. Tank—well, he just left. And my father is going to leave his money to the zoo—he says the animals are his true relatives—and to a foundation that's pledged to preserve the habitat of timber wolves. Twenty million dollars in all, and I'm—I'm going to end up with nothing. Nothing! And I can't find anyone to help me."

I mulled the situation over for a moment, then said, "Maybe what you need is an exorcist."

"I thought of that," she said with a sniffle. "The only exorcists in the city say they don't do werewolves, just demons."

"I don't do werewolves either, lady." I was beginning to get a very bad feeling about all this.

"I don't expect you to." She dabbed carefully at her eyes with a cocktail napkin, trying not to smear her makeup, then said, "Will you help me, Mr. Weatherby?"

"I can't answer that," I said. "I still don't have any idea what the hell you want."

"Oh," she said, back together now. She gave me a small, arid smile. "I'm not making myself very clear, am I? I'd like you to do two things, really."

"Yes?"

"First, convince my father not to disown me if I marry Worth, and—second, if possible, convince him that he's not turning into a werewolf."

"That sounds possible. What about Tank?"

"I'd like to know what he's doing, of course."

I thought about it all. Hell, not much of a job, really.

"I still have some money," she said. "About three hundred thousand from what my mother left me. I—I've given Worth about fifty thousand for some expenses that came up, but he's supposed to pay me back the first of the year. Look, Mr. Weatherby. If you can get Father's thinking straightened out and find out what's going on with Tank, I'll give you twenty thousand dollars."

I thought about it for another long three seconds before I said, "Miss Thaddeus, I don't know about your father. I'm not a psychiatrist, but I'll try. As for your brother—hell, that's easy."

"Then you'll help me?"

"Lady, you've just hired yourself a detective."

CHAPTER
SIX

THE HOUSE WAS A VICTORIAN MONSTROSITY SET ON grounds as big as the city park. It consisted of three decaying stories of brick and brown clapboard. Turrets, cupolas, and deep-set gabled windows loomed above eucalyptus, ironwood, and lemon trees. The gingerbread trimming hung loose in a dozen places.

I parked on the flagstone driveway beside a five-car garage with only an ancient navy-blue Edsel in it, the car's rear bumper held together with wire.

Tall, ragged hedges halfway hid the leaded panes of glass in a dozen dormer windows on the ground floor. Ivy grew in tangles up the walls. The house was imprisoned by foliage, cast in a perpetual twilight. The only splashes of color came from a sunlit patch of green shingles atop the house and from a brilliant fuchsia bougainvillaea bush beside the front porch.

I stepped up to the massive front door. A nasty-looking brass griffin with an open mouth sheltered the doorbell. I stuck my finger in, punched the button, and heard chimes inside as deep and heavy and slow as funeral bells.

A rustling came from one of the hedges off to one side. A small brown squirrel darted out, broke the silence by chattering angrily at me, then scampered up a tree. He seemed right at home. Probably one of the family.

I rang again and waited.

Footsteps.

The massive door swung slowly inward. A woman stepped out of the shadows.

Sixty years of gravity had given her doggie bags beneath her eyes and deep jowls, even though she was skinny. She had carrot-red hair, flecked with gray and cropped short. She glared at me with the most brilliant lavender eyes I've ever seen, the color enhanced by the broken red veins in the whites. The smell of alcohol wafted around her. Another one whose line was wine.

Her navy-blue nurse's dress hung almost to her ankles. The little Peter Pan collar was stained to yellow. She winged out her bony arms, planted her hands on skinny hips, and said, "Well?" in a voice like vinegar.

"Miss Partridge?"

She nodded.

"I'm Artie Weatherby. I believe Mr. Thaddeus is expecting me."

She gave me a withering look, pulled the door all the way open, then stepped aside. When she said, "Well?" again, I walked past her. She fell in beside me and jerked her thumb forward, saying, "This way." I followed her down the hallway.

The house was silent. There was a stale, musty scent of age over everything and, beneath that, another unpleasant odor I recognized. Cats. We walked past half a dozen closed doorways, beneath oil portraits of scowling people—probably Thaddeuses long gone, and good riddance. There were narrow dark oak tables set at intervals along the walls, with Oriental vases filled with dusty, dried flowers. When we reached the last doorway she stopped and gestured at me to enter.

Something scratched in the wall beside me. I stopped in my tracks. The sound got louder, a heavy clawing and scuffling behind the wainscoting. Then, just as suddenly as it had begun, it stopped.

Miss Partridge had been standing there, a look of disgust on her face as she gazed down at the wainscoting. Now she looked at me, scowled, and again said, "Well?" She jerked her thumb at the closed doorway.

I shrugged my shoulders, gave her a half bow, turned around, and opened the door. She snorted as she faded back up the hallway.

The large room was larded with the scent of Mentholatum. The space was so dim and musty that the shafts of light coming through the slightly parted curtains were brown. The long trip down the dark hallway had adjusted my eyes to the dimness. I could see a man sitting in a wheelchair against the far wall. He said, "Well, don't just stand there. Come in, come in."

I stepped onto the aged, flowered rug and walked past dark, massive chairs and sofas with wilted antimacassars on their backs. The furniture must surely have been reupholstered horsehide. Come to think of it, the scent of horses lingered still, just beneath the Mentholatum. There were plants everywhere, mostly large ferns, potted palms, and rubber plants. They filled every corner, sat atop hutches and tables, hung in a dozen places from the dark ceiling.

I said, "How do you do. I take it you're Mr. Thaddeus?"

He rolled his chair a few feet toward me. "Get over here, boy, where I can see you. How in the Cain and Abel am I supposed to know what to say to you when I can't even see who you are?" His voice was dry and scratchy as a cactus.

I stepped over to him. He looked up at me and squinted, then said, "Ah! Thought you were the good-looking one for a minute there. Glad to see you ain't."

"I beg your pardon?"

"The good-looking one, boy. One wants to marry my daughter? Says he's a big-shot doctor of some kind?"

I said, "I'm Artie Weatherby, sir. I called earlier."

"Well, whoever you are, looks like you're already here. Whatta ya want?"

"Sir, I was hired by your daughter to find your son. Tank."

He cackled, slapping his thin, bony hand on a knee beneath his lap robe. His laugh was a higher, shriller version of Tank's seal bark. His shoulders jerked up and down. I watched him in surprise. When he stopped laughing, I said, "I'm sorry. I seem to be missing something here. Your daughter told me to call you, said you'd like to see me."

He suddenly froze. "I'd like to see anybody, young man. Just anybody. My sight's going, you know."

I said, "Why don't we turn on some lights, maybe open those drapes and get some sunlight in here. That might help."

"You a smart aleck of some kind?"

I shook my head to clear it, and said, "Excuse me?"

"As if you didn't know." He was pouting now, petulant. Maybe he was senile.

I decided that if I was going to get anywhere at all, I'd better humor him. I said, "I'm sorry, but I *don't* know. Would you mind explaining what you're talking about?"

"The sunlight," he said. "You know damned good and well that I can't be exposed to sunlight. You pull those drapes and we'll see what happens, we'll just see! I suppose Jill put you up to it!"

Whoa, boy! This guy *was* strange. After a quick appraisal of the situation, I almost bolted. But the sudden vision of twenty big ones flitted across my brain. What the hell! I was already here. I might as well as least see if I *could* do the job.

I said, "Mr. Thaddeus, may I sit down?"

"Of course, boy. Be comfortable, be comfortable. Why don't you sit right here?" He wheeled over and patted the seat of a high-backed chair beside him.

I sat down. He rolled his chair a few feet away from me, rubbed his hands together, and said, " 'Well, now, here we are."

My eyes had adjusted a bit more and I was close enough to the old man to see a strong resemblance between him and his son, even though he was much smaller than Tank.

His hair was silver gray and unusually thick. It was cropped short on his head—probably the work of Miss Partridge, since it resembled her own haircut. He wore a brown house robe, and the backs of his hands were tufted over with thick gray hair that almost looked like fur. There were also tufts of hair in the indentation beneath his Adam's apple and above his collar. But his nails were immaculate and recently manicured. His clothing was old but clean. His eyes were the same olive green as both Tank's and Jill's, but there was a life in them that was missing in both of his children's.

His wheelchair had a tray attached, one of those contraptions you can swing around in front or else latch to one side. The only thing on it was a large bowl of rocks.

"Mr. Thaddeus, I understand you've been sick. I hate to bother you, but I've found your son. He's out in the desert, living in a small town called Desolado. Jill thought you'd like to know."

"Hogwash!"

"I beg your pardon?"

He said, "Jill sent you out to check on me, just like she sent that doctor. Go ahead, get out your camera. Take your pictures so you can laugh, just go ahead! My daughter thinks I'm going senile at best, plain stark raving mad at worst. I've got news for her, and most of it isn't good." He scowled suddenly at a corner of the room that was a tangle of lush plants. His eyes slitted and he yelled, "Hssst! Get out of there!"

I jerked my head around in time to spot the fattest cat I've ever seen scampering from behind a potted plant. She gave us both a malevolent look, then darted across the room and jumped right onto the old man's lap. The air went out of him with a *whoof*!

He didn't seem to mind. Instantly, he went to work scratching the fat old tabby behind the ears. The cat's purring soon made a background for his words. "Jill wants my money. Tank, as you call him, wants my—oh, ho, ho, oh—hah, hah, hah!" And off he went again, into gales of laughter that sounded like a demented seal's bark. The cat sat up and scowled at him for disturbing her, but he didn't notice.

When at last he stopped laughing and dried his eyes on the sleeve of his house robe, he said, "Excuse me, boy, but there's something about that name. Can't even hear it without laughing. Why would a boy with a good honest name like Abernathy want to call himself—hoo, hoo—" He caught himself this time, choking the laughter back in small sputters.

"Jill said the nickname was from when he played football in junior high school."

Thaddeus turned grouchy, squinted at me, and said, "Played football, did he? Strangest damned things happening around here and nobody ever bothers to tell *me*. Here, here! Get away!" His attention had shifted to something moving in another dark corner of the room. He lifted a small rock from the bowl on the tray and heaved it into the corner. Something scurried away. The light was too dim for me to see what it was, but I caught a disquieting glimpse of sharp little teeth and a long tail.

"Secret is to scare the little critters without hurtin' 'em," he said. "Anyway, my son wants my money, too—to spend on dope and no-good women. Thinks I don't know. Cut him off already, without a cent. My children are no good, Mr.—uh—what did you say your name was?"

"Weatherby. Artie Weatherby."

"Mr. Weatherby, my children are a couple of rotten, no-good, spoiled brats. Now that I'm sick and going through this strange transformation, all they can think about is getting me over the hill and into the zoo as quickly as possible so they can get to my money. By the way, what sort of doctor does my daughter want to marry, anyway? The kind that can stick me in the loony bin?"

"I'm afraid I can't answer that, sir. I've never met him, and she didn't tell me."

He narrowed his eyes, lowered his heavy white eyebrows, and said, "Now I'd call that strange all by itself, wouldn't you?"

I didn't respond. I couldn't think of anything to say.

It didn't matter to him. He had already picked up the conversational ball. "Going to get the best of both those kids, though. I'll tell you that much, Mr. Weatherby. Goin' to cut my daughter off without a cent if she marries that quack." He smiled with relish, then his face changed as he thought of something else. "Say, you like animals, boy?"

The cat still lay in his lap, purring, but I could have sworn it opened one malevolent eye and looked at me, waiting for my answer. I said, "Of course. Doesn't everybody?"

Thaddeus snorted disdainfully. "No, Mr. Weatherby, everyone does not. My daughter had a canary when she was a child. She let it escape and a cat killed it. Does that sound to you like everyone likes animals? When my son was eight, he traded his wagon for a BB gun and developed the horrible habit of shooting birds in the gardens. Does *that* sound like everyone likes animals, Mr. Weatherby? Does it? And my wife—my dear, departed wife—once dumped an entire bowl of guppies down the latrine, ferns and water and all. Said she didn't see the fish in there. Does that sound like the act of an animal lover? Can you imagine the fate of those poor creatures? Can you? The neighbors do their damnedest to make me get rid of half my pets, and mine is the only shelter they have from this heartless world. And my own children—" His look turned crafty and he said, "Well, my children would turn all my friends out of house and home if I let them. But they damned well won't get the chance."

"Mr. Thaddeus, I'm puzzled. I was led to believe that you were deeply disturbed by your son's absence."

"Ha!" He looked at me with contempt. "After he let my Siamese fighting fish die? After he harassed my hamsters half to death? I'd say not. Good riddance."

"Mr. Thaddeus," I said, "I hate to be nosy, but I understand you're ill. Would you mind explaining to me the nature of your illness? Jill is quite concerned."

"Hogwash, if the hogs will excuse me. Jill is concerned that I won't die soon enough for her to marry that namby-pamby quack of hers before he finds someone with more money. I may be old, but I'm not a fool. No sir, not a fool."

"What if he's not after her money? Some doctors do pretty well on their own."

"Hogwash. Why else would anybody want to marry that whiny little thing? Girl's got a personality like a hard-boiled egg. Besides, never seen a doctor in my life cared about anything but money."

"Mr. Thaddeus, you don't seem to have much confidence in doctors. Have you seen a doctor about your health?"

"Doctors be damned. All of 'em."

"Sir," I said, "are you—are you possibly—dying?" I didn't know how else to ask except to spit it out.

He snorted contemptuously at me and said, "Not altogether, boy. Come around at midnight on the next full moon and I'll be happy to show you just how dead I am." I could have sworn that the cat was smiling a deep, malicious smile.

I decided to backtrack. "Mr. Thaddeus, I was told that you *do* like animals."

"*Like* 'em? The worst animal is better than the best human being any day of the week, boy. Say, like to see some of my pets?"

I remembered the scratching in the walls, the fleeting glimpse of teeth and tail. "Just what kinds of pets do you keep?" I asked.

"Anything that needs to be kept, boy. I draw the line at insects. They'll take over if you let them. Say, I have a full-fledged zoo at the back of the estate. Care to see it?"

Quickly I said, "Some other time, sir." Then, remembering Jill's words, I added, "By the way, do you keep bats?"

He smiled and relaxed for the first time since I'd been there. "Why, yes, I do. You like them, too? Fascinating little creatures, aren't they? I have several different kinds, including some *Pipistrellus nanus,* rare little things only an inch and a half wide. Like to see them? They're right up in the attic."

Hastily, I said, "It's daytime. Wouldn't they be sleeping?"

He looked at me in amazement. "Why, I'll be damned. You certainly are a considerate young man."

"Thank you, sir. And thanks for your time, but I'm afraid I must be going."

"Well, it was certainly nice of you to drop by, Mr.—Mr.—What did you say your name was?"

"Weatherby. Artie Weatherby."

"Oh, yes. Well, stop by anytime, Mr. Weatherby. Come back sometime and see my bats."

"Yes, sir, I will. Thank you."

CHAPTER SEVEN

I DROVE SOUTH ON EL AGUA, TURNED LEFT ON QUAKER, and parked my car in the lot on the corner. The smell of the ocean hung heavy in the air. The gray waves chopped at the docks across the street. It was going to rain.

I walked past a used-record store, past a diner that gave off appetizing odors of fresh-brewed coffee and frying hamburgers, and into the lobby of the six-story square where I'd taken a year's lease on an office. Most of the tenants were either union or had something to do with shipping. There was one dentist in the building who had a steady stream of female clients—he did more abortions than extractions. The only other person on my floor was a bookie whose front was life insurance.

I hit the elevator button for the fourth floor.

When I walked in my office door, I almost tripped over a pile of mail beneath the mail slot. I picked it up, took it over to the desk, and thumbed through it. Ed McMahon was promising to send me a check for ten million dollars. I laid that one to one side. There were sales at every major store in town, and flyers in my mail for every sale. I tossed them all into the trash can. There was an advertisement for health insurance and another for magazines. I tossed them, too. That took care of the mail.

34

I turned on my answering machine.

The utility company had called about the bill; my land-lord had called about the rent check; a telephone solicitor had called about exercise equipment. The last message was from a woman with a high, reedy voice who identified herself as Marnie Evans. She wanted to hire a private dick. Was I available? Could I call her right away? I didn't.

I spent the better part of the next hour writing checks, dropping them into envelopes, then calling my various bill collectors and telling them the check was on the way. Then I kicked back and stared at the ceiling.

A spider was working on a web in one corner. I started to stand up on my chair and knock him down, then remembered that I'd seen a few cockroaches in the building. I decided to let him live. I wondered if old man Thaddeus would approve.

It started to drizzle. I swiveled my chair around to look out of my window to the docks. An oil tanker was berthed there. So was a barge. A huge, reptilian crane was unloading cargo containers, swinging back and forth with them in its teeth. The sky got darker. Rain fell. Across the small inlet to the north, I could see the rain-misted, crosshatched serpentine of the roller coaster towering above the shore. Some of the lights in the amusement park were blinking on.

I picked up the phone and dialed Jill Thaddeus. She'd worked me into a situation I didn't understand. Either everyone was crazy, or everyone was lying. It didn't matter which right then. I wanted to get to the bottom of things.

Her maid answered the phone and told me that Miss Thaddeus and her fiancé had drive up to Lake Folsom Point for the weekend. Would I like to leave a message? She sounded like a nice lady, so I didn't.

I kicked back in my chair again and stared at the ceiling. Nothing there but the spider working on his web.

The phone gave a little ring as if it were clearing its throat, then rang again. I answered it. "Weatherby Investigations."

It was the woman with the reedy voice. "Mr. Weatherby?"

"Speaking."

"You don't know me yet. My name is Marnie Evans. I need some help, sweetie. Are you busy now?"

"I'm working on a case. Could you call back in about a week?"

"Oh, no. I was so hoping you'd see me today. I have all these problems, sweetie, and I'm all alone here with nobody to help—and you won't even come over to talk to me? And I'd be *so good* to you, darling. . . ."

"Sorry. I have to go out of town."

"Well, darling, they told me you were hard to get. See? You're already running away from me."

"It's just that I have prior commitments." The truth and nothing but. I'd already decided to run back out to Desolado, kick over a few rocks, see what skittered out from under them.

"Well, you just run along and do your other things, darling. I'll be back in touch. Little Marnie doesn't give up when she wants something." She hung up.

Five minutes after her call, I'd forgotten her. I had my mind on the collection of Looney-Toons more formally called the Thaddeus family. I was getting damned curious about what really lay beneath the absurdity—damned curious.

The rain had stopped and left a thick wall of humidity. As soon as I'd climbed back into my car, I turned on the air conditioner.

I drove home and called the Lime County Car Rental Agency, then took a short nap while I waited for the delivery. I'd already packed my overnighter. A Hispanic kid about seventeen delivered a compact red Toyota. I dropped him back at the rental agency, then drove down Huntington Boulevard and hung a left at Crenshaw Street. I turned left again at Casaba.

I was in the small suburb of El Sereno—two-story brick stores, gas stations on every corner, palm, date, and pepper trees lining the wide streets. Kids on bicycles were coming home from school, zigzagging their bikes toward white frame houses with white picket fences and green, green lawns. *Leave It to Beaver* Land. At the end of Date Street, I swung right and entered the Escapado Freeway.

As I passed the suburbs, the streams of traffic began to thin. The debris of the outskirts fell away on either side of me: factories and warehouses, shopping malls, truck terminals, refineries, lumberyards, drive-in theaters, and restaurants, all linked together by an ugly gossamer of telephone and utility lines.

For an hour the freeway ate through low, rocky hills, dry earth, and dust. Then there was flatness and even drier earth, even more barren rocks sprouting saguaros and yuccas and sagebrush and Joshua trees, and then I was taking the southbound exit to Desolado.

I'd brought a couple of cassettes to help pass the time. I shoved a medley of Walt Disney tunes into the tape deck and whistled along with them. Whistle while you work.

I slowed down as I passed Sandy's Tavern and old man Tucker's store. I drove beyond the shacks and sheds and shanties that made up the town. Just at the south side there was a truck stop and cafe. It was just coming on dusk, that special desert dusk that makes you wistful and sappy.

There were two sixteen-wheelers parked in front of the cafe. Also two cars and two jet-black Harleys with the Satan's Sadists emblem on them. I parked my red Toyota beside the motorcycles and went in.

The booths were red plastic; the tables were gray Formica. The ceiling was water-stained. The Rolling Stones ground it out on the jukebox. The waitresses—both of them—wore white uniforms that had wilted with the heat. They looked disgusted with everything as they moved from table to table, from table to kitchen, and from kitchen to table. They had a tough life.

The waitress with the fresh-scrubbed face came up to the booth I was sitting in and handed me a menu. I studied it.

The truck drivers sat at the counter, talking about weights and tires and how to beat the Highway Patrol. An elderly couple occupied the booth next to me, looking tired and happy, talking about the grandchildren they'd just visited. A guy who bore the look of a traveling salesman sat in another booth, eating a hamburger.

My eyes stopped at the second booth from the back.

The woman was alone. She was a honey blonde, and she'd just taken a bite out of a grilled cheese sandwich. I stared at her. She lifted a big spoon to her mouth and nibbled at what looked like chili.

She had a golden tan and clear green eyes like emeralds on clouds. Long, dark lashes. Her honey-colored hair was a perfect complement to her tan. She wore a faded blue denim blouse that was unbuttoned a modest two buttons from the top, and her hair was combed straight back from her forehead, revealing a profile that would have made any New York fashion model go out and shoot her plastic surgeon.

She didn't even see me. She finished her chili, then dabbed at her mouth with a paper napkin while I sat and stared at her.

A man came out of the door marked MEN'S, swung into the booth, and sat down across from her.

I couldn't see his face, just the back of his head. He wore a grease monkey's hat turned backward. The hair that straggled out from under the hat was brown and dirty. When he turned his head a little, I could see a large diamond earring in his right ear. He wore a Levi's jacket with the gold, purple, and pink insignia of the Satan's Sadists on the back and sleeves. He said something to the woman, and her lilting laugh cascaded like liquid sunshine mixed with honey.

The waitress was standing beside me. "What'll it be?"

"I'll have the house salad and fried chicken," I said.

"With or without extras?"

"With."

"What to drink?"

"Iced tea."

"That'll be extra, you know."

"Fine."

She went away. I took a long drink from the warm glass

of water she'd put in front of me, then again turned my attention to the honey blonde.

She and the man were standing up, getting ready to leave. As she rose, she caught me staring. Her eyes narrowed suspiciously for a second while she sized me up, then she smiled warmly, so warmly that her companion whipped around and shot me a scowl. He was big, maybe six foot four. His face was long, lantern-jawed, and leathery from too much time in the wind and sun. His pale eyes were too large for his face. Lines etched around his mouth told me that he probably had a cruel streak. He focused on the woman and raised his eyebrows questioningly, but she was looking back at him now, smiling serenely. He relaxed.

As they walked to the cash register and paid the bill, I got a better look at her. She was slender, yet with the rounded curves of a milkmaid. Her faded pants matched her shirt and had grease on them. She wore heavy biker's boots. A red, grease-stained handkerchief hung out of her back pocket.

A biker's broad. Damn! Why did she have to be a biker's broad? Of all the women in this world, they had to be the most screwed up.

Their men beat them, whipped them, used them, turned them out on the streets, made them sleep with other members of the clubs—yet you couldn't pry most biker's broads away from their men with wild horses and motorcycle chains. And I'd never met one yet who hadn't been strung out on drugs. Not that the drugs were the only reason they were screwed up. Clean them up and you were still likely to have a serious masochist on your hands.

Too bad. That was one gorgeous woman.

As they walked to the door, she glanced at me once again and smiled fleetingly. Then they were outside. Seconds later, I heard the Harleys growl to life.

The waitress set my fried chicken and salad in front of me and asked, "Anything else?"

"Maybe a new world," I said.

"Huh?"

"Never mind. Could you tell me how to get to the Cactus Corners Motel and Garage?"

"Shoulda asked that guy that just left. He owns the place."

"Yeah?"

"Yeah. Nails McNulty. Easy enough to find it, though. Head on south for half a mile. You can't miss it. Leastwise, you'd better not. It's the last stop between here and the border."

CHAPTER
EIGHT

THE MOTEL OFFICE WAS JUST BIG ENOUGH TO HOLD THE narrow, chest-high counter. It had a bell on top of it with a sign: PLEASE RING.

I did.

The woman who came through the doorway from the inner room was thick and old. She had a smaller version of Nails' lantern jaw and the same pale fish eyes.

"Do you have a vacancy for the night?" I asked.

She appraised me, then said, "Single?"

"Yes, please."

"Just one night?"

"Yeah."

"With kitchenette?"

"I won't need one. Have to take off early in the morning."

"Going across the border?" Her interrogation was a bit too casual.

"Just into Desolado again. Trying to make a couple of insurance sales."

That satisfied her. She looked at me and said flatly, "That'll be cash in advance." I paid her, took the key she handed me, then walked back outside.

The motel consisted of a double row of faded pink stucco

41

cabins set in a large grove of gnarled, thirsty cottonwoods. Bare bulbs hung above each doorway. I drove my red Toyota down to the end cabin and parked it. I was opposite a cabin with two hot-pink mopeds in front of it and a stripped-down silver Harley beside it. There were lights in the cabin windows.

To the south was a small, lighted swimming pool—bait for weary travelers. Beyond that was the desert night, with its haze of stars.

To the west of the motel was a large, white-washed cinderblock building. I'd seen the white sign with its black block letters as I'd driven in: CACTUS CORNERS GARAGE— Body Shop, Engines Overhauled, Motorcycles Customized, Brake, Tune-Up and Muffler. On its far side there was a wide junkyard, hidden from the highway by a corrugated iron fence, a full acre of dead, dismantled, wrecked, and mangled cars and motorcycles. There were dusty cottonwoods throughout the car and bike graveyard.

Behind the garage was a large wooden shed. Lights glowed from two high windows. Halfway between that and the motel was a ramshackle house with a sagging roof. There were lights on there, too, and several cars and bikes were parked in front. I could hear the sounds of a television.

My room was depressing: threadbare carpet, sagging bedsprings, noisy plumbing, and mold. The sheets were rough and stale, and I hoped I was the first one to sleep in them since they'd been washed. I unpacked my overnighter, then took a shower.

I set my alarm wristwatch for midnight, climbed into the sack, and fell asleep. When the little beep awakened me, I rolled out, rinsed my face with cold water, tugged on Levi's, an old shirt, socks, and sneakers. I took my police flashlight out of the suitcase and attached it to a belt loop, then checked my .38 Chief Special and slipped it into my shoulder holster. I pulled on a worn Levi's jacket, left my bedside lamp burning, and slipped out the door.

The lights were still on in the unit across from me. That seemed like a good place to start. After all, I was being paid to find out what Tank Thaddeus was up to, wasn't I? And whatever he was doing, at that moment he was most likely doing it in there.

Careful to avoid the gravel in the driveway, I moved along the grass at the edge of the cabins and around the silver Harley. I crept to the back of the cabin and stood on tiptoe. I was six inches too short to see in the window.

I turned the flashlight on low and looked around at the junk and car scraps. There was a sawhorse behind another cabin. I went over, picked it up, carried it back, then climbed up on it.

I was looking into a small kitchenette. White enameled cupboards, a small table covered with a red-and-white-checked oilcloth. A warped, brownish yellow linoleum floor. The refrigerator was so old its shoulders were rounded, and the stove was one of the narrow kind. I could see partway through the kitchen door into a tiny living room. Someone's large, booted feet were on a rickety coffee table. I could hear tinny laughter coming from a TV, then Johnny Carson's voice saying something I couldn't make out, and then there was laughter again.

Bunny came through the kitchen door so unexpectedly that I instinctively leaned back from her. I lost my balance.

I caught myself by leaning forward fast. I hit the wall with a faint thud.

Bunny stopped, cocked her head to listen, a frown on her face. Then she shook her head as if to clear it and moved on to the refrigerator. She opened the door, took out two cans of beer, then went back into the other room. More tinny laughter.

I'd been holding my breath. After letting it out in a long, silent stream, I stepped lightly off the sawhorse and carried it back to where I'd found it. I crouched into the shadows behind the vacant cabin and waited.

Not a sound.

No doors opening and closing, no one coming outside. The stars gleamed in the clear dark sky, and the chill made me appreciate my jacket. There was a pungent fragrance of sage and sand on the night air.

I checked my watch. I'd been there for twenty minutes.

Careful to stay in the shadows, I edged along the buildings, then darted past the automobile skeletons to the back of the garage, where the wooden shed showed light.

To the left of the building was a pile of tires. Silently, I rolled four of them over and beneath one of the high windows, piled them one atop the other, then lifted myself up to stand on them.

My nose was pressed to a grimy window. The room was large; the walls were rough wood. Bare bulbs hung from the rafters. A cluttered workbench ran along the left wall. In the back, fifty or more cases of paint were stacked, some of the cans sitting outside the boxes. There were half a dozen people inside, including the honey blonde and her fish-eyed boyfriend, Nails McNulty. They were drinking beer as they watched two men work on a new Jaguar.

The car, parked in the middle of the room, had been sanded down. Masking tape covered the windows and the chrome. Chunks of paint-stained tarp covered the tires. One of the men wore a painter's mask. He hit a switch, then turned the nozzle of a paint spray gun on the car. It began to turn a deep maroon.

So they were painting a car. So what? The sign on the garage had said body work. Maybe they were ambitious, working nights to get ahead. As Abernathy Thaddeus II would have said, hogwash! They were operating a chop shop.

They probably ripped off the cars in the city, brought them out here at night, filed off the engine numbers, repainted them, supplied them with titles from other cars that had been wrecked, then shipped them far, far away—for a healthy profit. *That* was why old man Tucker had asked if my BMW was stolen! He probably . . . Something grabbed my legs.

Tires flew out from under me, rolling off to every side as I fell. Someone let out a long, low laugh as I hit the ground. I caught myself in time to jackknife away from a heavy boot flying into my face. The Old Special Forces training and my time in Nam served me well now and then.

The big door to the shed burst open and I was lying in the middle of a square of light. People were running toward me, yelling and talking, but I had my hands full with the steel mesh of arms and legs trying to pin me, collapse me, crush me.

Something crashed into my chest—a knee—then another punch glanced off my chin. I tried to go for my gun, but someone grabbed my legs from behind again and I fell forward. Another boot crashed toward me and I jerked aside, just in time to keep it from crushing my jaw.

I broke away with a few zigzag motions and rolled to my feet. I had just gained my balance when the army of arms and legs was on me again. Whatever it was, it was big and it had a lot of limbs.

I pulled my face back from another punch and let fly one of my own that made a mushy, crunching contact. Then someone grabbed me from behind again. There were four of them on me now, and two more waiting for a chance to jump in. One of them held a huge wrench.

I jerked back from another punch, spun around in a side-snap kick. I could see Tank Thaddeus in the mêlée now, a dull, angry expression on his face. The girl must have heard me after all.

Just as that fleeting thought passed, another blow landed from behind, this one in my kidneys. I tried to spin again, but the wrench came down and caught me dead behind the ear. I was through moving for a while. I folded to the dirt.

CHAPTER NINE

A SURGE OF PANIC SWEPT ME UP AND OUT FROM UNDER the dark waves. I couldn't move my hands. The VC had attacked; shrapnel had blown my hands off; something had fused my arms together. There was a tap-tap-tapping as someone came closer.

I tried to open my eyes. They were weighted down with lead, but I finally got them open. I was looking at a boot, tapping on the floor beside my ear. I looked slowly up and into the face of the honey blonde. She put a finger to her lips, warning me to silence. I stuck out my tongue and licked my lips. Bloody, but no gag. Where I'd been, I hadn't been able to do much talking. Behind her, I could see the newly painted Jag. The smell of fresh paint was mixing with the taste of fresh blood to make me sick. The side of my head ached and throbbed.

I swallowed hard. I could make out the sound of flies buzzing now, then my head cleared some more and the buzzing began to separate into voices. Swiftly, I tried to move my hands again.

They were bound tightly, the rope twining all the way up to hold my arms out stiff like the shanks of a butchered beef hanging from a slaughterhouse hook. My shoulder joints ached.

46

The woman looked me over, shook her head in disgust, then said, "Wait."

Considering the options I had, it seemed like an odd command. I bowed to necessity and waited.

My legs were cramping and my mouth was full of blood. I tried to turn over enough to spit, but the woman, her body suddenly tensing, whispered again, "Wait."

I rolled my head, spat the blood onto the floor, then muttered, "Wait for what?"

"Shh!" she cried, but it was too late.

Tank Thaddeus's voice cut through the flies. "He awake?"

They'd been right behind me, outside. He stepped in, grabbed my collar, and tried to lift me up like a sack of flour. My head was about two feet above the concrete floor when my shirt collar tore. My head hit the concrete with a melonlike thud. Sparks flew on the inside. Thaddeus laughed.

He leaned over again. This time he picked me up beneath my arms and dragged me out the door. I was on the ground again, bathed once again in the square of light. Someone said, "He's a narc."

"Shaddup," said Tank.

Bunny's voice whined, "Kill him, Bay-bee! He'll snitch on us. No matter who he is, bust his head open. He'll snitch on us, Bay-bee!"

"Shaddup, Bunny," said Tank.

Then another voice cut in. "Canyon will be out soon to pick up his money. Let's wait till after he's gone. He has too much on us already. Too many ways to get in on the cash."

"Uh—right, Nails," said Tank.

There were several of them on me again, picking me up, dragging me up a short flight of steps. They dropped me on a threadbare bile-green rug. "Now get to work on the Volvo," said Nails.

"Uh—uh—right, Nails," said Tank.

"I says we kill him now," someone grunted. They were behind me, and I couldn't see who was talking.

"Shaddup, Stinky," said Nails.

"Stinky's right," said another voice. "It's stupid to wait."

"Greasy," said Nails, "I ought to snuff you and Stinky. Lester the Molester, too. If you guys had been on guard like you were supposed to be, this wouldn't have happened. So just don't start trying to tell me what to do. This is my garage and I'm the president here. Don't you forget it!"

"What about Snake?" Greasy wailed. "*He* was supposed to be watching the garage. Where was he?"

A new voice growled, "He 'uz tryin' out the coke stash we jes' got up from the Mexes. Got hisself coked out. Heh."

"Shaddup, Jonesie. All of you, all of you, just shaddup! Let's get to work on the Volvo. We ain't got much time afore the Mexes get back." In unison, they all said, "Right, Nails."

"I'll keep an eye on him," said the honey blonde with the honeyed voice.

"Right, Crystal," said Nails.

They tramped out the door, then there was a long silence. And then Crystal was bending over me with a long, sharp knife in her hand.

I yelped.

"Shut up!" she said. She eyed me critically while she went to work cutting on my ropes. As she sawed away, she said, "What in hell *are* you doing out here, anyway? They're planning to kill you, you know."

I was too amazed to say anything.

She seemed irritated with herself. She said, "Don't ask me why I'm getting you out of this. Nails is going to be mad as hell at me again. But I just can't let them do it. Frankly, I wish I could. Look, as soon as I get these ropes off, I want you to run out the back and hide in the junkyard. Wait until the uproar dies down, then look for a junked-out cherry-red Mercedes. There's a big hole in the fence right beside it. That'll get you through to the irrigation ditch. Then turn right. Keep going until you get to a big culvert. Hide in there. I have to make a coke run into the city about noon. I'll pick you up and take you with me. Make sure you wait in the culvert. I'll honk four times.''

My wrists were almost free. "Come with me," I said. "Get away from this place. These people are losers. You're too good to be here."

"I can't."

I couldn't hide my jealousy. "Why not? Can't you stand to leave that schmuck Nails?"

The last thread of rope around my ankles came loose. She stood up and her voice turned icy as she said, "I'm not really with him, you know." She looked at me like I was something she'd just scraped off her shoe. "Look, whoever you are, if you want to live until morning, you'd better get the hell out of here. Canyon'll be here any minute. As soon as he leaves, they'll be back here checking on you."

I kicked the last strand of rope off my legs as I said again, "Come with me. I don't want you to get hurt. Look, my name's Artie Weatherby. I'm a private investigator from the city. I can help you."

She shook her head impatiently. "Get out of here. Canyon will be here any minute."

"Come with me. Please. I won't go without you."

She rolled her eyes toward the ceiling. "Why me?" Then she looked back at me, her eyes hard, and said, "Okay, stay. They're only going to kill you. Bury you in that ravine over there. What the hell? Why not stick around for the excitement?"

"I'll go if you'll go with me."

Chivalry is dead. She reached inside the back of her Levi's waistband and pulled out a gleaming .45. She aimed it straight at me and said, "Run, you mother, or I'm going to shoot you myself!"

She meant it. She *really* meant it. What the hell! Maybe she could take care of herself; maybe she was one of those women who could bring home the bacon, fry it up in a pan. . . .

I was looking down the barrel of her gun. She clicked

back the hammer. I shrugged, then turned and sprinted out the back door. She followed me.

I took one more look at her, then started jogging through the sagebrush and over the raw earth.

Something went flying past my head. It landed in a clump of sagebrush up ahead of me. I veered over and stooped to see what it was.

She'd thrown me my gun.

CHAPTER
TEN

JUST ABOVE THE HORIZON, A HALF MOON HUNG. THE stars were bright, glistening drops of light against the oily blackness of the sky. I'd barely reached the first hunk of metal when car lights swept through the gate in the corrugated iron fence and pulled up in front of the house where I'd left Crystal. Bikers came out of the shed. I heard voices, greetings. Then Crystal came out to the porch.

Nails leaped up the steps and took a step toward her, raising his hand as if to strike her. Her head jerked back and instantly she had her gun leveled on him. He dropped his hand, his shoulders sagged as she said something, and then he turned back to the short, squat man who'd climbed from the car. Nails motioned for him to come inside.

I was crouching. Now I ducked past the hunk of metal I'd been hiding behind and started to move past all the skeletons lying around me like victims of some vast metallic cataclysm. They were thrown every which way, decapitated, disemboweled.

Motorcycle lights were coming on, engines revving up. I climbed into the back of the junked-out red Mercedes and watched. Bike lights crawled out of the yard; some of them spread in different directions, while others began combing

the road. They were looking for me. Lights went on in the
motel office. A moment later, lights went on in my cabin.

I waited. After maybe an hour, the motorcycle lights had
either reentered the yard and been extinguished, or they'd
blazed off down the road toward town. Sheriff Bryce Canyon had climbed back into his car and sped away. Two
figures who looked like Crystal and Nails came walking
out of the house, seemingly friends. They went into the
shed.

Somehow, she'd thrown them off my scent.

My watch said four-thirty. Not long before dawn. It was
so cold that a faint rime of frost had formed on the car
windows. Time to move.

I climbed out of the Mercedes and felt my way carefully
along the fence. I found the hole. It was close to the ground.
I fell to my belly and crawled through. On the other side I
tumbled through tall weeds, past rough brush, and then I
was at the bottom of a four-foot-deep irrigation ditch. No
water in it, thank God.

The ditch ran alongside the highway. The brush was hip-
deep, while the ditch itself was deep enough so that only
my head and shoulders protruded over the top. It was getting colder. A faint wedge of daylight shone on the horizon.

I plowed through the brush and weeds, my pants getting
soaked from the morning dew. My foot hit something
bulky. I tripped and half fell by landing on something soft
and strangely familiar. An unpleasant smell wafted up from
beneath the brush and weeds.

Pushing myself upright, I pulled the weeds and grass
apart, tore a mass of tumbleweeds from atop the brush, and
stared downward.

It was old man Tucker.

My hand had landed on his chest. His head was turned
at an incongruous angle. The back of his head was caked
with blood, and there was a smell now of the onset of
decay.

The corpse was clad in a blue denim work shirt and
matching pants. There was an old, worn wallet in the hip

pocket, holding the usual identification and two twenty-dollar bills—probably the same ones I'd given him. The card I'd asked him to give to Tank Thaddeus was gone. Folded into the money compartment were two magazine pictures, full-color glossy ads. One was for a new Ferrari. The other, for the Islands Vacation Club, showed a bevy of bikini-clad girls looking worshipfully at an old man in a bathing suit and shades, his little potbelly spilling out as he lounged in a sunchair, sipping a drink.

One of Tucker's arms had been broken. There were welts on the side of his head, and bruises had had time to form on his arms and throat before someone had laid a blow that had caved in his head. My hand crept to the back of my own head where it had encountered a pipe wrench a scant few hours before. It was still so tender I involuntarily jumped when my fingers made light contact.

Back to Tucker. Someone had tried to make him talk before he'd been killed. The beating he endured made that a virtual certainty. Well . . . No point in notifying the sheriff or anyone else, at least not until I got back to the city.

I suddenly wondered if Crystal had sent me this way on purpose, if she'd known that old man Tucker's body was here. With that woman, who could tell? Who knew what she was capable of?

The sun was coming up. And a distant growl told me that something was coming down the highway. I dropped into the weed-filled ditch, then peeked back out.

It was an oil tanker, coming up from the border. Unlikely that the Sadists had managed to commandeer that.

I scrambled up the bank, stuck out my thumb, then tried my boyish grin on the man behind the wheel. It hurt my lips to make a smile.

I thought for a minute that the trucker was going to pass me, but he yanked on the air brakes. I sprinted down the highway as best I could to where he'd finally rolled to a stop. He leaned over and opened the door for me, saying, "Buddy, you look like you just crawled out of a meat grinder. What the hey happened to ya, anyway? Car wreck?" He clamped a cigar back between yellowed teeth and motioned me in with a broad hand attached to a thick, tattoo-covered arm.

I nodded in agreement. "I was driving with a suspended license. Didn't want to call the police."

He flashed me the same kind of grin that Oilcan Charley used to give to fair maidens, then said, "Welcome aboard. Closest hospital's back in the city, but I'm goin' that way. Happy to take ya there, if ya live that long."

I settled myself into the seat, gave him another of those painful grins, then said, "Thanks." But the word was lost in the grinding of gears as he shifted and hit the gas pedal. The truck growled back onto the highway and down the road.

CHAPTER
ELEVEN

HE DROPPED ME AT A TRUCK STOP ON THE EDGE OF town. I caught a cab and went home.

I showered, cleaned my wounds with peroxide, then fell into bed. At eight o'clock I woke up, the pain in my kidneys still raw, and couldn't go back to sleep. I ate half a papaya, and some wheat toast, washed down with a cup of tea. Then I went out, got in my BMW, and drove to the office.

They were waiting for me. I saw them as soon as I climbed out of my car and started up the street. They weren't even trying to hide.

They were sitting in a gray car, government-issue, across the street from my office building. As I got closer, I could see their faces, one Hispanic, one Anglo, both chiseled into determination, one in a brown suit, the other in blue.

As soon as I opened the lobby door to step into the foyer, they were out of the car and right behind me, one on either side, following like fins on a fish.

I stepped into the elevator. They followed. I pushed the button for the fourth floor. They didn't push anything. I turned to them and said, "Good morning, gentlemen." The Hispanic looked at the floor; the Anglo stared straight ahead.

They followed me out of the elevator, down the corridor, and waited while I unlocked my office door. I held the door open to them. The Anglo reached into his pocket and pulled out a shield holder, flipped it open to display a badge.

Surprise! I'd thought they were city cops. The badge explained it: U.S. Department of Justice, Drug Enforcement Administration. DEA.

I bowed from the waist, stood aside, and motioned for them to precede me into the room. The Anglo said, "Smartass, ain't he?" His partner said, "Never met a private dick yet that wasn't."

The Hispanic man in the brown suit had liquid brown eyes that any woman would have been jealous of. He didn't bother with a handshake but said perfunctorily, "I'm Special Agent Tafoya. This is Special Agent Taft. We don't have much time."

"Good," I said. "I'll try not to take any more of it than I have to."

Taft was in his mid-forties, and he looked as tough as a Mafia hit man. His stiff hair was flecked with gray, and his eyes were brown and hard. He was a study in contained tension and repressed anger. He looked at me with contempt, and as he spoke he weighed every word.

"Mr. Weatherby, we understand that you spent last night at the Cactus Corners Motel and Garage, just outside of Desolado."

How the hell did they know that already? Were they psychic?

I said, "I guess the sheriff picked up my rental car? I forgot that I'd rented it in my real name."

"Rental car?" It was Tafoya, talking to Taft.

Taft waved the question away. "What were you doing down there?"

"Trying to get some sleep," I replied.

"Smartass," said Tafoya to Taft.

Taft nodded, then said to me, "Are you working on a case?"

"I am."

"Who's your client?"

"You know I can't tell you that."

"By hell, we can take you to court and drag it out of you," Taft said.

"Look, hold on," I said. "I don't know what's got you so upset, but yes, I am working on a case. A small missing-persons thing. I was sent by a woman to find her brother, who happens to be living near Desolado with the Satan's Sadists. Frankly, I went down there to spy on him. The bikers caught me, tied me up, beat the hell out of me in the process, and I got away. Anything else you want to know?"

Taft looked at Tafoya and said, "That fits with what we've got."

Tafoya nodded.

Taft said, "We're going to have to ask you to give up the case."

I looked at him, shook my head slowly, and said, "Uh-uh. I have twenty thousand dollars riding on this case. I'm not giving it up."

They looked at each other, suspicion lighting up both sets of eyes, and Taft turned back to me. "You've got a twenty-thousand-dollar fee coming just for solving a missing-persons case? Get serious, shamus. The lowest con on the totem pole could think up a better one than that."

"It's true."

"Who's your client? Daddy Warbucks looking for Little Orphan Annie?"

"I'm not at liberty to say. You know that."

"You watch too much TV, Weatherby. We'll have you up before a grand jury before lunch. Who the hell's your client?"

"Look," I said, "put me up before a grand jury. I *love* being important. But I'll tell you one thing. There's a body in an irrigation ditch about a half mile east of the garage. It's old man Tucker, Uriah Tucker, who owned the store next to Sandy's Tavern in Desolado."

"You kill him?" His hands were already going for the cuffs.

"No. Hell, no. Look, they nabbed me while I was peeking into their window. The Satan's Sadists are operating a chop shop out there, probably a cocaine drop, too.''

They looked at each other swiftly, real concern in their eyes.

I said, ''They tied me up. There was a girl out there named Crystal. She helped me get away.''

''Helped you get away?'' said Taft stupidly.

''But—?'' said Tafoya.

''Shaddup,'' said Taft.

I said, ''There's a chop shop, a coke drop, and a dead body out there in the desert. I hate to sound like every other spineless citizen you mess with, but with all that work to do, why are you hanging around here picking on me?''

Tafoya gave his partner an inquisitive look. Taft clenched his teeth, then said, ''Let's take the chance. Tell him.''

Tafoya nodded, said, ''Right,'' then turned to me, a steely look on his face. ''Mr. Weatherby, you've fallen into the middle of one of our undercover operations.''

My disbelief must have been apparent, because Taft said roughly, ''Oh, yes, shamus, you tried to screw things up good. The Satan's Sadists bring in an estimated fifty to seventy-five million dollars a year in illegal substances— methamphetamines, cocaine, heroin, illegally produced Quaaludes. You name it and they deal it. Desolado is only a part of their operation.

''We have more than a year invested in this operation. We aren't about to let you blow it. No matter how much cash some nit is willing to hand to you to find one of those slimeballs.''

Tafoya said, ''We want you to butt out.''

''Let me think about it.''

''*Think* about it?'' Taft leaned toward me, his fists balling up and his face turning even colder.

Tafoya leaned toward him, raised a cautioning hand, and said, ''Now, Fred, don't lose it. We can handle him in other ways.''

Taft growled, ''This asshole wants to *think* about it? While we've got people's lives on the line out there?''

"I'm not an unreasonable man," I assured them. "Maybe we can work something out."

"Work something *out*? Shamus, you're dealing with the U.S. Justice Department. We don't make compromises." Tafoya glared at me.

Taft said, "We aren't going to be jacked around. We want you to stay out of Desolado. You're interfering with a government operation."

I said, "Well, I'll see what I can do. I'll have to talk to my client."

They shot each other swift, dark looks, and Taft said, "You sure as hell don't plan to mention anything we said here to your client, do you?"

"Look," I explained, "all dicks aren't dicks."

Tafoya nodded, and Taft stared at the floor, still an exercise in sustained tension. Tafoya said, "All right, Mr. Weatherby. I suppose we can't hold you responsible for what's happened so far. It's not your fault that you stumbled into our operation. But if this leaks, we'll definitely know where to plug the leak—if you catch my drift. We'll have you behind bars for a long, long time. Do I make myself clear?"

"Clear as the outline of that popgun under your jacket."

"He's a smartass," Taft said. Tafoya nodded. "Stay out of Desolado," Taft continued. "We've got some heavy things coming down down there, and if you screw them up, you're liable to accidentally get in the way of a bullet. We wouldn't want that, would we?"

"I don't know about you," I said, "but I wouldn't."

"Then stay the hell out of Desolado," Taft said.

They turned, like Tweedledum and Tweedledee, and walked out the door.

CHAPTER
TWELVE

I THOUGHT ABOUT WHAT THEY'D SAID FOR A FEW MIN-
utes, then I picked up the telephone and called information.
When I had the right number, I called Desolado.

"Cactus Corners Motel." The voice belonged to the old
woman who'd checked me in the night before.

"Who am I speaking to, please?"

"This here's Mrs. McNulty"

"Is Mr. McNulty there?"

There was a long pause, then she said, "Who the hell
is this? My old man took a lam on me fifteen years ago.
What the hell you tryin' to pull?"

"I was asking for your son, ma'am."

"Oh, Nails," she said. "Why didn'tcha say so? Who
the hell is this, anyway?"

I said, "John Dougherty, ma'am. I have the red Toyota
that was left at your motel last night. I got to partying with
some friends, and—well—I ended up back here in the city.
I'd like to come and pick it up. I left a few things in the
motel, too."

"What in hell you tryin' to pull? I ain't never seen no
red Toyota here. What's this poppycock about the motel?"

"John Dougherty? I checked in last night."

"You're full of it, fella. Only customers we got last

night was a trucker and a couple of oldsters on their way back from visitin' their grandkids. What you tryin' to pull? Got me a mind to call old Bryce Canyon. He's—''

''Yeah, I know. He's the law in your parts.''

''Damn right.'' She hung up.

Next, I called the Lime County Car Rental Agency and told Julio, the owner, that his red Toyota had been stolen the night before, in Desolado. He growled for a while, then told me he'd send a cop later to take a report. I told me never mind, I'd drop by downtown.

Next I called Jill Thaddeus. Her maid asked me to wait for a minute, then the breathy, finishing-school voice came on the line. ''Hello?''

''Weatherby here. We have to talk.''

''Oh, no. Not—uh-not now. Can't you call back?''

''It's important.''

''I—I can't talk now.''

I heard a man's voice in the background, calling, ''Who is it, dear? Is it the hospital?'' She evidently cupped her hand over the mouthpiece, because her voice was muffled, and she called back, ''No, dear, just a—a telephone solicitor.''

In a strident whisper, she said to me, ''I have to go. I—I'll phone you as soon as I can. But whatever you do, don't call back here!''

''I'll keep our little secret,'' I promised.

I was very popular on the telephone that day. I decided to call my old buddy over at the *International Inquirer*. Maybe he'd want to talk to me.

The front desk put me through to him and he answered the phone, ''Angelo here.''

''Hey, old buddy,'' I said. ''It's about that hundred you still owe me.''

''Weatherby?''

''How many people do you owe money to, anyway?''

''Plenty,'' he said sadly. ''Look, Weatherby, I can't pay you now, but you know I'm good for it. With six kids— well, Linda had to have braces and we didn't have any insurance—''

"I'm going to let you pay me anyway," I said. "I need some information, and it's worth a hundred bucks to me."

"You're on."

"I need it ASAP. Maybe by tomorrow morning?"

"Anything's possible. Shoot."

I described Taft and Tafoya to him, then asked him to do a tracer on them. "Are you nuts?" he exclaimed.

"Of course I am. Why do you ask?"

"They're feds, Weatherby. Feds, as in federal agents. Why in hell are you mixed up with them?"

"I just need to know if they're crooked or clean, Angelo. Crooked or clean."

"And they're drug enforcement, you say?"

"Right."

"Hell, Weatherby, how am *I* supposed to find out in one night if they're crooked or not?"

"Just get what you can. You know a lot of people. Ask some questions, find out what kinds of reputations they have, what kinds of cases they work on, who their connections are—that sort of stuff. Dig through your archives and see what they've done in the way of drug busts."

"I know how to run an investigation, Weatherby. I'm a reporter, remember?"

"I remember. I thought you'd forgotten."

"Screw you."

"I'll get back to you first thing in the morning," I said, then hung up before he had a chance to.

I swiveled my chair around so that I could look out over the bay. A tugboat was guiding a barge into port. I watched them for a while, thinking, then I dialed Jill Thaddeus again.

She answered the phone. "Oh, it's you again. I was hoping you'd call."

"Wha—?"

"Worth was here and I couldn't talk," she said. "I need to see you. Have you had dinner?"

"Not yet." I felt confused.

"Let's see. . . . Worth never goes to the Hotel Irvine.

They've got an excellent dining room. Could you be there in, say, an hour?''

"Your wish is my command," I said.

I let her hang up first.

CHAPTER
THIRTEEN

THE HOTEL IRVINE'S DINING ROOM WAS ONE OF THOSE places where a tuxedoed maître d'hotel meets you at the door simply to sneer at you. Then another tuxedoed man comes up behind him and takes you to your table.

I got a few dirty looks as I walked through the room—my shark-blue sports jacket and white pants weren't quite ritzy enough for the champagne-and-pinched-nostrils set—but I made it to the table without any serious meltdown from the withering stares.

Jill Thaddeus was already there—at a table in a private corner. She looked expensive, in a slate-blue cocktail dress with a diamond necklace and matching earrings. Her auburn hair was brushed back, held up by a diamond pin. It was a cosmic puzzle how anyone that attractive could be so unappealing. Her father was right; she had the personality of a hard-boiled egg.

I bowed slightly, then slid into the chair across from her. I said, "Glad you could make it."

"Oh, well," she said vapidly, "I had to eat, too. The escargots here are excellent. They make a nice spinach salad, too."

Spinach and snails. That was, of course, exactly the kind of food she'd eat.

I said, "I went to see your father."

She honored me with her arid smile and said, "Did you see his bats?"

"Not yet, but I've been invited to."

She looked down into her champagne glass, swirled the liquid around, then said, "Can you do anything about him?"

"I'm working on it."

She looked at me gratefully, laid her eyelashes down on her cheeks a few times, then nodded. Her imitation of a man trap.

I said, "There's something that bothers me, though."

"Yes?"

"What if he really *is* turning into a werewolf?"

Her shoulders slumped. Her mouth turned down at the corners. "Things are bad enough without your making fun of me."

"Your father seems to have a few screws loose," I said, "but to tell you the truth, I like the old guy. He insists that you and Tank are both trying to take his money. What do you say about that?"

She looked at me worriedly. "Poor Father. That Miss Partridge is at him all day long. She's a drunk, always tugging at a bottle of wine. She makes him think the strangest things. I am truly worried about him. I—I've tried and tried to get him to see a doctor, but, well—"

"Isn't your fiancé a doctor?"

"Well, yes, but he's not exactly the one to treat Father. He doesn't like Father, for one thing. Father was just furious when Worth went out and took those photographs of him and—well—"

"Your father says that your fiancé is just after the money, too. That *all* doctors think of nothing but money."

"That's ridiculous. Worth is a rich man."

"You told me you'd lent him fifty big ones."

"Big ones?"

"Fifty thou."

"Oh, that. He has all his money invested. He lives off

the income. He—he ran short, is all, and didn't want to divest any of his capital. I just loaned it to him until he gets his next dividend check.''

"Dividends from what?"

"Well, really, Mr. Weatherby, he didn't say, and it's not the sort of question you ask someone.''

"Even if you're going to marry them?"

"He's a rich man. He just bought a brand-new Mercedes, and—well, Mr. Weatherby, I didn't want to tell you, but the fifty thousand went for this engagement ring.'' She flashed the diamond my way. "That is, part of it did. He wanted me to have it right away.''

"Why can't you talk to me when he's around?"

"He—he doesn't know.''

"Know what?"

"About us. That we're seeing each other. He's very old-fashioned.''

"Miss Thaddeus, ours is strictly a business relationship. There's no reason he shouldn't know about it.''

"He—he wouldn't approve.''

"Of what?"

"Of my relying on you instead of him.''

"Your father thinks he might be considering having him committed to, in your father's words, a loony bin. Is it possible?''

She looked astonished. "That's the most ridiculous thing that Father has come up with yet! Surely you've heard of my fiancé? Dr. Worthington Sterling?''

"Nope.''

"Worth is the most prominent plastic surgeon in the city.'' She swelled up proudly. "He's done half the breasts and noses in town.''

"Sorry, I guess we travel in different circles. This is the first time I've heard of him.'' Sheesh! A knocker doctor. Well, at least he wasn't some quack who was going to put the old man away and marry the fair maiden's money.

The waiter came with Jill's snails and spinach and my Caesar salad. When he'd gone away again, I said, "Miss

Thaddeus, you hired me to track your brother. I owe it to you to tell you that he's in a lot of trouble. It would be good if you could talk him into leaving Desolado and coming home. He has some serious problem with drugs, and he's getting in deeper and deeper."

"But I thought you would get him to come home."

"Wrong. I was hired to find out what he's doing."

"What is he doing, exactly?"

"He's probably doing a lot of cocaine and PCP, Miss Thaddeus."

"What else?"

"He's living in Desolado with the Satan's Sadists."

"Oooh! You *are* impossible! Is that—the awful girl still with him?"

"Girl?"

"Yes—uh—Bunny. It's all her fault, you know. If Worth hadn't introduced them—"

"Wait a minute. Hold on. I'm completely lost now. Why don't you go back to the beginning and tell me everything. And try not to thread in too many lies. I'm having a hard time working around them."

"I guess I might as well tell you."

She dabbed a tear from her eye with the dinner napkin, then said, "I never really knew my father well. Or Tank either, for that matter. I was away at school after Mother died. When I came home to visit, it was as if I was among strangers. And I think I knew even then that my family was—well—strange, not like other families. Father was already obsessed with his animals, and Tank was already rebellious.

"I think it was because of Father and Tank, but I was never comfortable around men. I didn't date much in college. When I graduated, I came back here. With the money Mother had left in trust for me and the money Father gave me, I lived very well. That's when I met Worth." She frowned and unconsciously twisted at the engagement ring. "He was quite a darling with all the girls at the country club, you know, and—well—I find this difficult to talk about—"

"Talk anyway," I said.

"I'd—I'd considered having a breast lift." She blushed deeply. I managed to keep from laughing. "I—all the other girls were having them. Everyone said to go to Dr. Sterling, that he was the best man in town."

"So, to make a long story short, you went."

"Yes," she said, still blushing. "But he wouldn't perform the operation. He said—" She cast her eyes away from me. "He said I had the most beautiful breasts he'd ever seen. He refused to do a thing to them except—" She blushed deeper. "Well, we were engaged that same month."

"What do Bunny and Tank have to do with all this?"

She looked in my eyes again. "Why, Worth is the one who introduced them. I thought I'd told you. He's the surgeon who performed the operation on—on Bunny, of course."

"Operation?" I was thinking of her enormous breasts.

"Why, yes, of course. The sex change."

"Sex change?" A mouthful of salad fell to my plate.

A small smile took some of the frost off her face. "Why, yes. You must have seen her. You mean you didn't know?"

"She looked like the real deal to me."

"Amazing, isn't it? Worth is a very talented surgeon."

A sudden thought came to me. "So, then, if that's the case, is Bunny really your brother's girlfriend? I mean, boyfriend? I mean—does he—or she—or whatever—do they—?"

"Yes, they're lovers."

"Then that means that Tank isn't really as macho as he pretends? That he's—he's—gay?"

"Frankly, Mr. Weatherby, it's been my unfortunate experience that many of the most macho men are gay. I mean, they hate women, don't they? But my brother is *not* gay. Worth thought it would be funny to introduce him to Bruce—I mean Barbara—I mean *Bunny* McNulty right after he—er—she got out of the hospital. Worth was proud of his work, you know. He wanted to see if Tank could tell. I'm afraid Tank fell head over heels. Now he flatly refuses to believe that Bunny is anything but a real woman. That's the main reason he took off out to the desert and won't come back."

The old brain sent out a red alert. "You've tried to *get* him to come back?" I asked.

"Well—I—well, yes."

"Then you've known where he was all along?"

"Really, Mr. Weatherby, this whole thing is quite confusing."

"You're telling me! I thought you hired me to find him."

"I didn't mean to lie. What I wanted was to know what he was doing."

I was getting a strong feeling that she knew at least part of what was happening at the Cactus Corners Motel and Garage. And that led me to another question. Why? I asked her. "Why? Why does that concern you so much? What do you think he's up to? And why is it so important to you?"

She said, "Tank says he's in love with Bunny. He wants to marry him—uh—her. Father and I are distraught. Simply distraught."

Red alert. Whatever her father was, he was definitely not distraught.

She looked at me sadly. Her two well-manicured hands moved up to cover her mouth. Two huge teardrops rolled down her cheeks. She sniffled, then wailed softly, "Oh, Mr. Weatherby. How can I explain it to you when I don't understand myself? I'm afraid! Something terrible is happening. You must help me. You have to get Tank to come home before it's too late." Her voice trailed off into a sob.

More drama? Somehow I didn't think so. I reached across and took her hand. It lay in my own like a cold, dead fish. I said, "I'll do what I can, Miss Thaddeus. I promise."

She refused to let me take her home. Worth might bump

into us. I saw her to a cab, got into my own car, then drove home.

Now what to do?

Cracker Jacks. That whole family—the whole case, for that matter—was Cracker Jacks.

I uncapped a bottle of mineral water, poured it into a glass, added ice, squeezed in some fresh lime, then carried it onto the patio. I sat down, propped up my feet, and looked down the canyon to the wedge of light that was the city. A hot Santa Malo wind blew across from the desert and up through the canyon.

Nothing seemed to fit. Still, I tried to piece everything together.

I had a madcap millionaire who was turning into a werewolf and who liked his pet animals better than his own kids—not that I really blamed him. His daughter was lying through her teeth half the time she talked, but was still desperate enough to offer me twenty thou for leg work and amateur psychology. The son had a grease-and-drug-impacted brain and associated with some society types who recycled stolen cars and imported enough dope to create permanent brain damage in half the kids in the city. Add to that one sex change, a couple of feds, one honey blonde who trafficked in cocaine but still took time to perform acts of mercy, and you probably couldn't get the picture either.

It all added up to one of Hieronymus Bosch's nightmares.

And then there was Uriah Tucker. Or, rather, the *body* of Uriah Tucker. Who killed him? The bikers? Why? Had the woman called Crystal known his body was in the irrigation ditch when she'd sent me that way?

Suddenly I got a dark premonition about her. Whatever was going down, she didn't belong there. She was too human, not yet numbed out from the violence and the drugs.

When I dreamed that night, I was slaying a small, spiteful dragon with a face like old man Tucker's with fish eyes and wisps of scraggly yellow-gray hair. He had a fair, honey-haired maiden chained to a motorcycle. On the horizon, a whole menagerie of animals sat watching the three of us. I kept getting the feeling that they wanted the dragon to win.

CHAPTER
FOURTEEN

FIRST THING THE NEXT MORNING, I CALLED ANGELO again. "Hey, old buddy. Did you come up with that information?"

"Weatherby?"

"The same. Learn anything?"

"Nothing you're going to like."

"Well, fire away anyway, as we used to say in Nam."

"Do you recall that ten-million-dollar heroin bust last year, the one called Operation Brown Sugar? Where they busted the mayor of that border town, Nuevo Codicia?"

"Yeah, I remember. Was that Taft's baby? Tafoya's?"

"Both of them. They're a tight team."

"You dig up any dirt on them?"

"Hell, Weatherby, from what I can see so far, they're the fair-haired boys of the whole damned DEA. They seem to have the juice to back up anything they want to do."

"There's nothing at all? Not even a hint of anything crooked?"

"Weatherby, what the hell is this with you? Why is it so important to dig something up on these guys? You working for the drug traffickers now?"

"I don't know, Angelo. There's just something about the two of them that doesn't jibe. They're sweating too

72

hard over a very slight contact I had with one of their undercover operations. You check everything you could?"

"Weatherby, I've been up all night. I've been through the archives for the past ten years, on the phone to everybody in the press *and* in law enforcement who ever owed me a favor. You got your money's worth." He hung up the phone.

I didn't like it. Those two were up to something. I needed to lay some more background into the puzzle. I was in the process of figuring out how to do that when my phone rang.

"Weatherby here."

"Good morning, darling. It's little old me again."

She'd caught me off guard. "Little old *who*?"

"Don't be such an old grouch. It's me—Marnie. I still need a big, blue-eyed private eye to come over and solve my problems. Are you busy, sweetie?"

"Up to my armpits." What the hell was this woman up to?

"You naughty boy, you've been hiding from me."

"I've been working on a case. I still am."

"You are so *mean*!" she squealed. "Will you come and see itsy-bitsy me? Please? I'll be *so* grateful."

What the hell? "How did you know what color my eyes are?"

She giggled. "Marnie has her ways."

"What do you want?"

"I want you to help me."

"Help you what?"

"You are *so* mean. I have a problem that can only be solved by a big, tall, blue-eyed private eye."

She had me curious; I'll give her that. "I have some paperwork to catch up on today," I said.

"Come and visit itsy-bitsy me tonight. I'll make us some din-din."

"I might be able to get away for an hour or so."

She squealed, "Oh, how wonderful! Can you be here at eight?"

I thought about it, then said, "I should be able to make it about then."

"Oh, I can't wait. I'll fix us something very special."

"Don't bother on my account."

"It's no bother, darling. It will be a pleasure."

I wrote down her address.

"See you at eight, blue eyes," she cooed.

CHAPTER
FIFTEEN

I STEPPED OVER TO MY BMW AND BENT TO UNLOCK THE door.

They'd been waiting for me, one on either side of the pepper trees. They approached, guns drawn—regulation governmental tactics. Taft moved in closest, and I felt the round metal of a gun barrel against my ribs. He said, "Well, well, if it isn't the brilliant Mr. Weatherby." He pulled my .38 from my shoulder holster. "I'll just relieve you of that gun, shamus."

Taft gestured with his .45. His face was white with tension. He said, "Our car is just beyond that grove of trees. How'd you like to go for a little ride?"

"You're taking me for a ride? I thought it was the guys on the other side who did that."

"Smartass, isn't he?" Taft said to Tafoya. Tafoya nodded. The gun barrel dug into my ribs, and Tafoya said, *"Move!"*

I climbed into the backseat of their gray Plymouth. Tafoya plopped beside me, pushing me over to the far door, and Taft squeezed behind the steering wheel. "Am I under arrest?" I asked.

They ignored my question. Tafoya kept his gun dead on me.

Taft backed out from behind the trees. "Let's just take him up the canyon a ways," he said. "Say five miles or so. This is the last house in the canyon."

I was starting to get a very queasy feeling.

They didn't say a word as we drove higher into the canyon. Up past the scrub oak and dried foliage. I felt cold shivers running down my back. They were going to kill me. . . .

"There's a good spot," said Tafoya.

Taft agreed. He turned off the road and into the trees. As he slid from beneath the wheel, he took his gun out, too. Tafoya was already out, gesturing for me to emerge.

Taft said, "You sure we're far enough away for the gunshots not to carry?"

Tafoya looked hard and said, "No problem. I brought my silencer."

"Too bad this asshole was such a slow learner," Taft said. "He coulda been a good man if he'd had time to grow up."

Sweating, I said, "Wait a minute. What's the problem? What did I do?"

"What did he do, he wants to know!" Taft smirked to Tafoya. "What did he do? The guy's not only an asshole. He's a whiner."

"But—but—I—"

"We told you to butt out," Taft said.

"You didn't," said Tafoya. "You called the Cactus Corners Motel first thing after we left. And then you started asking questions all over town about us."

Lamely, I said, "I just wanted to get my car back."

"Oh, yeah? That why you started attracting all that frigging attention to us? So you could get your car back?"

I said, "I just—" and Taft, his fist powerful as a wrecking ball, whacked me right in my gut. I doubled over and would have lost my breakfast if I'd had any.

I don't give up easily, especially when two men with guns are getting ready to kill me. I said, "Look, you guys—" and Taft caught me in the side of the head with a karate chop that felt like a lead pipe. I staggered back and forth like a drunk, then crumpled to the ground.

They both scowled down at me. Taft said, "Hell, I wanted to do it with him standing up, sort of like a military execution. We're government. We're entitled to that, aren't we?"

Tafoya answered, "Man, don't you sometimes feel you'd like to get some of the crap these amateurs put us through out of your system?"

"Damned right," Taft growled. "Let's shoot him."

"Sure, we can shoot him. Empty both our guns into him if we want. Who's to stop us? But somehow, that just isn't enough."

"I see what you mean. These small-time assholes run around sticking their noses into everything and they don't care a rat's ass if they get every frigging one of us killed, so long as they make their frigging twenty-thousand-dollar fees."

"Damned right," said Tafoya, and he kicked me in the gut.

I'm good, but so were they, and it's hard to beat those odds—two men with two guns, both of them just as professional as I was. I got in some good punches, but these guys were lethal. It was an atonement with them, almost a religious experience. Catharsis. They worked me over systematically. Punches to the kidneys, chops to the groin—they especially seemed to enjoy slamming their fists into my gut, watching me double up. And every time I thought I might nail one of them, a gun barrel suddenly found its way into my face or to my temple and the thought of bullets ripping through bone and brain stopped me short, convinced me to take another of their blows. These guys were street fighters, dirty players. And they were killing me, beating me to death. . . .

Taft stopped first. Just like that. Right after one blow that brought me to my knees again, he stopped and said, "That's enough."

"It's your party," said Tafoya. "You still want him standing up?"

"Damned right," Taft said. "Military-style execution."

Tafoya pulled me up. I hung against him like a sack of potatoes, unable to stand up by myself. My guts had waves of fire in them. Blood streamed into my eyes and I couldn't see anything. I slowly pulled up one arm. It was like climbing a mountain. I wiped some of the blood away. I don't know why, but I wanted to see what was coming.

Tafoya shoved my arm back down. My knees sagged again.

Taft was standing dead ahead of us, his gun aimed and steadied with both hands. He said, "Can't say I'm sorry to have to do this, Weatherby. Hell, agents are getting killed all the time because of hotshot amateurs like you. Tell you the truth, it feels kind of good to get even. We're taking things into our hands, shamus. From now on, when things go down like this, we'll just nip the problem in the bud."

My lips were so stiff and sore I could barely move them to talk, but I tried anyway. "I—I didn't realize."

A cold glint came into Taft's eyes. He was pulling back the hammer on the gun, slowly, carefully, his tongue flicked out and licked at his lips. He held his aim steady, pulling slowly, slowly on the trigger.

My heart stopped beating as I watched.

Click! The gun fired on an empty chamber. With an evil grin, Taft threw the gun up in the air, caught it, twirled it around on his finger a few times, and said, "Surprise, shamus!"

Tafoya let go of me. My knees sagged and I crumpled to the ground again. Tafoya said, "The big bad feds aren't going to kill you *this* time after all. Just a little object lesson, to let you know we're serious."

"This is the last time we're telling you to butt out," Taft growled. "Next time, it's the real thing."

Both of them were smiling evilly as they climbed back into the car. They drove away and left me there, doubled up on the ground.

CHAPTER
SIXTEEN

AFTER MAYBE AN HOUR, I COULD SIT UP. THEN I COULD walk. I had to stop and rest a lot, mostly because of the cramps in my gut. Even so, it was only noon when I got back to my house.

I took a shower, then checked the bruises, scrapes, and cuts. I put on peroxide and a couple of bandages, then collapsed on to my bed.

It was nearly seven when I woke up. I was feeling a lot better. I thought about things, but nothing made any more sense than it had before. I'd already known that Taft and Tafoya were overreacting. They hadn't clarified anything for me. Damn. Maybe I needed a break from it all, a nice, weird evening with the owner of the high, reedy voice. I got up, patched myself together, and got dressed.

Marnie lived in one of the more elegant condominium projects on upper El Borracho Drive. You know the kind of place, a circular drive in front with a parking valet to take your car, large terra-cotta urns on either side of the door with giant ferns in them, a carpeted lobby, murals of cupids and clouds and Greek nymphs and satyrs. . . .

The security guard looked up from his newspaper as I came in. I gave him Marnie's apartment number. He pressed the intercom and announced me, then directed me toward the elevator.

She was waiting at her apartment door—a woman who was a perfect match for the high, reedy voice. "Oh, sweetie," she cried, "I'm so glad you could make it!" She preened for me.

She looked as if she'd been auditioning for a remake of a Jean Harlow movie, all four reels wrapped up into one bundle of pulsating pulchritude. She wore silver high-heeled shoes and a billowing, floor-length negligée of some creamy, translucent fabric with silver threads through it. Her nails were long—probably those silk things they put on these days—and painted a pale lavender. She had diamonds on every finger, including the pinkies, and she fluttered her hands around a lot so she could throw off sparkles of light. Her breasts were entrapped in a bodice with silver flowers on it, and they were trying hard to escape. Her lips were painted the same color as her nails. Her cheekbones were elfin-high, and above them her eyes were as big as a starving doe's. Her silver-blond hair was piled high, and she'd dusted it over with some kind of glitter.

The effect wasn't really Jean Harlow. She looked more like an anemic Christmas tree.

When she saw the bruises and cuts on my face, she gurgled, "Ooh, you naughty boy. Were you fighting? You just come in here, sweetie. Marnie will make you all better."

I stepped inside, handed her my jacket, and was suddenly overwhelmed by the cloying scent of roses.

I looked around for the roses. There wasn't a trace of a fresh flower anywhere in the room.

She'd set the table with candelabra. The candles were already lit. The rose smell was stronger now. Maybe it was her perfume?

She said, "Make yourself at home, sweetie."

I sat down on a white-and-gold brocaded love seat.

The apartment was expensive. There were crystal figurines everywhere, several good French Impressionist oils on the walls, a real fireplace with a white marble mantel, and one of those gold and crystal clocks on it. There was an oil portrait of an old, jowled man on one wall. The carpet was the same pale lavender as her nails and lips. There was a balcony with latticework doors opening onto the lights of the city, and just this side of the balcony was a formal dining room.

She came over to me, batted her eyelashes, then leaned over, pressing into me. Her perfume was a good, French musk. Not rose-scented.

I was uncomfortable and already regretting my decision to come here. My gut had begun to ache again, and I was having waves of dizziness. Maybe a slight concussion. I wanted to get this over with. I said, "Miss Evans, you said you wanted to see me professionally?"

She pecked me on the cheek. "That can wait, darling. First we'll have some din-din and get acquainted."

"I don't think I can eat much, if anything. My stomach—"

She ignored me. "Would you like a cocktail or champagne?"

"Do you have any Pepto Bismol?"

She giggled. "Oh, sweetie, you have *such* a sense of humor. And good-looking, too, aren't you. We'll have champagne. It fits my menu so perfectly. Why don't you go ahead and sit at the table? Yes, right there. That's where the head of the house should sit. It's where my late husband—"

"You're a widow?"

"Oh, yes, sweetie." She'd pushed in a big silver serving tray and deposited something into my dish. "That's his portrait on the wall. He was a sweetie, too, and *so* generous—" She smiled at me with capped teeth so white they reminded me of Chiclets. "Well?" she said.

"Well what?"

"Aren't you going to eat?"

"I'm sorry. I'm not feeling good."

"Try it, darling. It's watercress and sea lettuce. My own recipe."

I took a bite and chewed just to get her off my back.

She beamed, then started chowing down like a lumberjack. When her plate was empty, she swept my still full salad plate away and replaced it with something else. The smell of roses wafted up, filling the air. I swallowed hard and said, "What is it?"

"Baked roses, darling. A real delicacy! There are red roses, pink ones. White and yellow. They're stuffed with pine nuts and baby raspberries. Oh, darling, you'll just love them. Here, let me put some rose-flavored sauce over them—" She went to work with the ladle. "Now eat, darling."

I said, "You sounded pretty adamant on the telephone, or I wouldn't have come. I don't mean to be rude, but I'm not quite ready for dinner." I eyed the baked roses, sniffed them, and felt my stomach turn over.

"Oh, sweetie, after all the trouble I went to?"

"Sorry," I said. I was turning green. "Look, maybe I should come back another time?"

She dabbed at her lips with a napkin, sighed, and then in an eye blink dashed around the table and snuggled in my arms. I had to brace myself to keep from being toppled over. I felt a serious wave of dizziness sweep over me.

Taft and Tofoya had scrambled things up good inside me.

"Oh, sweetie," she purred, "I knew it would be like this."

I eased her over and onto a settee. I got down on my knees in front of her, because that was the most comfortable position for me. "Mrs. Evans, there seems to have been a misunderstanding." And then for some reason I remembered a little speech from *The Late Show*. "Some things are too precious to be rushed."

Her eyes narrowed and I thought for a second that she was getting mad. "I have to go," I said. I tried to stand up, but little washes of dizziness kept holding me down. Lamely, I added, "I'm not feeling well."

"Did you drink too much before you got here?" She eyed me hopefully. "Was that why you didn't want any of Marnie's yummy champagne?"

"Something like that." I made it to my feet, then reeled back into the wall.

She said, "My! Aren't we walking funny?" Things were a little hazy, but I thought her eyes narrowed thoughtfully as she said, "You'd better come into the bedroom and rest for a bit, sweetie. Come on. Right this way, darling. Here we go." She helped me onto the bed, then turned around and left.

The room had green brocaded wallpaper, green chairs, and a green bedspread. I felt color-coordinated, too. I made it off the bed and into a little pea-green bathroom, where I managed to splash some water on my face. I felt a little better.

I wanted to get out of there. *Bad.* When I don't feel good, I'm like a wounded animal. I don't want a lot of people around staring at me—I want to crawl away and lick my own wounds.

I made another start for the door, felt faint, and detoured onto the bed. Fatigue hit me like one of Taft's fists.

I passed out.

Something was walking across my nose.

In that haze between sleeping and waking, I brushed at it. My hand made contact with something solid.

"Ouch!" It was Marnie's reedy voice. "Oh! You are *so* damned mean!"

I opened my eyes to find her curled up next to me. She was leaning on one elbow, glowering down at me. Evidently, my hand had just made contact with the sides of her head. Streamers of her silver-blonde hair were still tickling my face.

Groggily, I said, "Sorry. I didn't know it was you. Thought it was roaches or something."

Her eyes narrowed up in anger, and as she spoke I realized she was now drunker than a loon. She said, "I was thinking about you, all alone in this big, old bed, and Marnie wanted to play. I'm sorry if I frightened you, sweetie."

Suddenly I knew I wasn't feeling any better than before I'd passed out. The baked roses were still rich in the air. Whatever Taft and Tafoya had done to my insides, it had started to ferment. A locomotive had leaped the tracks and run across my gut, then come back for a second run at my head.

And Marnie was serious about playing. The water bed was swaying as she rubbed into me. Her tresses skittered across my face like bugs on a marathon. She'd renewed her perfume, put on something with a rose base this time.

My stomach started to say hail Marys.

I tried to sit up. She mistook the motion for acquiescence. Suddenly she was all over me, ripping back the covers, pushing her breasts against me and grinding her ample hips.

My stomach turned over once.

She started to move rhythmically, trying to get me turned on. The water bed started to slosh back and forth.

My stomach turned over again.

She pulled my mouth to her ear, panting, "Oh, sweetie, Marnie wants you to bite her ear. Do it, sweetie, bite it!" She tackled my neck and pulled my nose and mouth directly to her ear.

My nostrils made contact right at the point where she'd dabbed on her rose perfume.

My stomach turned over for the third time and tried to escape through my mouth. I shoved her away and raced for the bathroom.

I was in there for a good fifteen minutes, what with refreshing myself with cold water. When I returned to the bedroom, all the lights were glaring. Marnie sat on the edge of the bed, bare-ass naked except for her silver bedjacket and silver high-heeled mules. One foot was tapping nonstop against the carpet. I mean, she was *mad*!

I tried to explain. "Look, it wasn't just you."

"Get out!" Her teeth were clenched together as she said it.

"I'm really sorry."

"Get out of here." Her eyes were colder than the ice swan at a gourmet feast. Her face was drawn as tight as beef jerky and as white as whipped cream.

"I didn't mean to insult you," I said, and she stood up and pointed at the door.

"Okay," I said, "I'm going."

She glowered at me as I pulled on my socks and shoes—she'd evidently taken them off. As I stepped into the second loafer, she said, "How dare you? I've never before in my life had a man puke when I was making love to him. How dare you?" There was murder in her eyes.

I buttoned my shirt as fast as I could. "I'm going, I'm going. But to tell you the truth, you brought this on yourself. I tried to tell you I was sick. Besides, call me old-fashioned or something. But I'm tired of cheap thrills in the backseat of Daddy's car."

She took off one of her silver mules and took aim. "Get out, get out, get out, get out, get out!"

"No problem," I said as I whipped through the bedroom door and into the living room. "And better luck to the next cat you try to poison."

I managed to slam the door behind me.

CHAPTER
SEVENTEEN

I WENT HOME TO BED, WHERE I SHOULD HAVE STAYED
to begin with.

The next morning I woke up sore and tired, mostly tired
of being dumped on. I started to get incensed. There's
nothing like a little pain to convince somebody that it's
time to kick ass.

Except that I wasn't big enough to kick both Taft's and
Tafoya's asses at the same time. They were as tough one
at a time as anyone I'd ever come up against. What I was
having trouble figuring out was why were directing all
that toughness at me.

And how in hell did they always know so much about
what I was doing? Hell, they must have known I'd been in
Desolado before I even got back to the city. And they'd
known, within hours, that I'd called the Cactus Corners
Motel and that I'd been trying to get a handle on their
backgrounds.

I called Angelo. "Hey, old buddy. Our two friendly
neighborhood feds worked me over yesterday. They found
out I made a phone call to the Cactus Corners Motel shortly
after they left. Got any ideas how that could have happened?"

"Bugs," said Angelo.

"Bugs?"

"Bugging devices. They might have your phone bugged. Or mine. Or maybe the motel's?"

"The motel's! That would make sense."

"What about yours, Weatherby? If they have yours, they're listening right now."

"Yeah, they would be. But I'll bet you hit the nail on the head when you said the motel. Look, Angelo, can you dig up anything else on them? Anything that might tell me why they're so damned stoked up about my little trip out to the desert?"

"Weatherby, your time is up. You got your hundred dollars' worth. I hit every base. What can I say? If you ask me, I'd say the guys are clean, but mean."

"Angelo, they worked me over. Feds aren't supposed to do that stuff. Their job is to collar people who do."

"You watch too much TV, Weatherby."

"So you're worried about them having my phone bugged and you have a wife and six kids to support. So you're tossing me to them."

"Yeah, that's the way I look at it, too. So what? You know, Weatherby, sometimes you're an all right guy."

"Forget it, Angelo. Look, if you won't help any more on that angle, do something else for me, huh?"

"Let's see how sane it is before I commit myself."

"You ever hear of a guy named Worthington Sterling? He's a doctor, a plastic surgeon."

"He's big money and as smooth as satin. And he's a complete flake. One of the guys here did a story on him last month. The man's had a dozen lawsuits brought against him in just the last year. The word is that he used too much anaesthetic on one woman who was having a nose job. It left her in a permanent coma. She damn near died right in his office."

"Office?"

"Well, yeah, sort of. He has one of those clinics. He was never nailed for that one that I know of, but he's being sued now for a tit job that went sour. Sagged down to the poor woman's knees. And Larry—that's the hack who's doing the stories—he did another article on Sterling about three months ago. A woman was suing him for doing a chemical peel that left her looking like Vincent Price in *House of Wax*.''

''Hell, the guy must be famous. Why haven't I heard of him before?''

''C'mon, Weatherby, this is all page-eight news. Only mob murders and nuclear attacks get the front page these days.''

''Can you tell me anything else about him?''

''Not much more off the top of the old bald noggin. But I suppose I *could* take time away from my neglected wife and my children with all their decaying teeth to—''

''There's another bill in it if you can help me out.''

''Consider it done.''

''I'll get back to you, then. *Gracias, amigo*.''

''Same to ya.''

Next I called Jill Thaddeus. Her maid told me she was out. Would I like to leave a message? I didn't.

I showered and shaved, then drank a bottle of mineral water. Fortunately, some of the knots in my gut had dissolved. I climbed into my car, drove to the Chick-n-Briskets, had a fried ham and egg sandwich, then drove south and east, to the Thaddeus estate.

Miss Partridge's doggie bags were several days lower on her face. Her breath was sour with yesterday's alcohol. She didn't want to admit me, but I pulled rank by shoving past her. I went down the hallway to the same room where Thaddeus had been before. It was empty.

Miss Partridge sneered at me and said, ''Well? Whattid ya expect, ya come bargin' in here like that?'' She sneered harder. ''He's upstairs, third door on the right.''

The old man seemed pleased to see me. ''Hello, Mr.—uh—what was the name?'' He was in a big brass bed, reclining against pillows.

''Weatherby. Artie Weatherby.''

''Ah, that's a good name. A good name. Hope you'll forgive me for not getting up, but I had one of my spells again last night. Full moon, you know. Takes a lot out of me.''

He did indeed seem subdued today.

I said, ''No problem, Mr. Thaddeus. I won't keep you long. I just need to ask a couple of questions.'' I sat down on a ghastly purple love seat with legs that looked like club feet. The tabby scurried out from under it, stopped to glare at me, then hurled herself up onto the pillows beside Thaddeus. His head bounced hard as she landed.

The house was quiet. The only sound was the old man's breathing, a heavy, belabored inhalation followed by a quick wheeze as he exhaled. He took a bite of something from atop a bed tray, chewed at it languidly, then swallowed. He had deep blue circles under his eyes, and I could have sworn that the tufts and clumps of gray-white hair were thicker than they'd been the last time I'd seen him. He'd grown a beard.

Something clawed at the floorboards right beside my chair. I froze. Looked down. Nothing there.

There was a sudden hollow scrape, then a scuffle, then the clawing came again—from inside the wall. Soft, at first. Then suddenly the wall came alive with scraping, scuffling and tearing. I jumped to my feet with a heavy thud. The noise stopped.

Thaddeus giggled, then let out a long, slow tee-hee-hee that brought Miss Partridge bustling through the door, hands on hips. Thaddeus clasped his hands over his mouth like a young boy, stifling the laughter.

Silence.

Miss Partridge scowled and glared around the room, fixing that glare on me for an uncomfortably long time before she scanned the shadows beneath plants, the undersides of the furniture, all the while staying fixed in that same spot.

Another sudden scuffling, louder than before. I moved gingerly to the middle of the room, then looked around me, first one way then the other. The noise grew louder. It was coming from all four walls now.

A fat black cat that I'd never seen before came scurrying through the open bedroom door. It shrieked, I jumped aside, and it lunged at the wallboard right beside Thaddeus' bed, hissing and clawing. Thaddeus yelled hoarsely, picked up a rock from a table beside the bed, and hurled it at the cat, shouting, "Hsst! Get of of here! Out! Miss Partridge, get that damned cat away from here. It's going to start a—" The tabby jumped from his pillow.

It attacked the walls, too, scratching and meowing at the wallboard, mewing and *pfff*ing, bouncing off first one wall then the other. The bedlam from within the walls was getting worse.

Miss Partridge stood in the middle of the room, still glaring, until her eyes seemed to blaze red. I stood, too, stone-cold still.

Another cat scurried through the open door, this one a white Siamese. I spun around as she bounced off the walls, setting the others back in motion. Then another cat bounced through the door. Another . . .

They were all mewing and caterwauling, all running about madly, bouncing off the wallboards. The scratching and scuffling in the walls had reached a furious intensity to match that of the cats, and I could hear faint squeaks now. Also tiny sounds like wood being gnawed through.

Cats were bounding across my feet, howling, tearing at draperies, and trying to climb them, flying from chair to chair . . .

Thaddeus shouted, "Miss Partridge, get these damned cats out of here!" He sat straight up in bed, glowering at all the darting, scampering, howling little beasts, and tried to shout above the cacophony and confusion and chaos: "Hsst! Scat, damn you all, scat!" He picked up a handful of pebbles and threw them at the white Siamese.

The cat leaped up on his dresser, pawed through dust-covered bottles and brushes. Thaddeus howled, "Scat, you crazy cat!" He threw more pebbles.

The cat leaped just in time, landing on all fours on the floor. The pebbles flew into the mirror, shattering it with a furious crash. Pandemonium.

White-faced, Miss Partridge stood in the midst of it all. Finally, as if she'd at last reached her limits, she screamed,

"Your fault!" She was facing Thaddeus now. "This is your fault, every damned bit of it!

"So! Insects are the *only* things that'll take over if you let them, eh? Well?" She was so agitated that she stomped over and kicked one heavy black shoe into the nearest wallboard, setting the scuffling in motion again, and screamed, "Stop it! That's enough now. Do you hear?"

The noise in the walls instantly stopped. Silence again.

The cats backed off, tensed up and ready to spring. They watched Miss Partridge with their crafty little feline eyes. She stood there, her cheeks puffing up with rage, her eyes flashing and then she couldn't contain herself anymore.

She flew into a frenzy. She stomped around the room, kicking the wallboards yet again, screaming, "Think you're hiding, huh? Think I don't know you're still there? I'll get you one of these days, you little bastards. I'll show you how to make life miserable."

The cats had all backed into one corner to get out of her way. They watched her curiously and then she saw them. She flew at them screaming, "Scat, scat!" Her arms flew like windmills. The cats looked at one another, then turned in a unit and bounded out of the room.

Only the tabby stayed. With a malicious twinkle in her eyes, she jumped back up onto the pillow beside Thaddeus, who lay back down. He clutched at his heart.

I started to move quickly to his side, but Miss Partridge was there first, shouting, "Laugh, will you, you old coot? Think it's funny? Just you wait until the typhoid comes along again! Funny! One of these days I'm going to get rid of your pets. You mark my words." I realized then that Thaddeus was grinning from ear to ear. Tears of laughter streamed out of his eyes.

Miss Partridge glared at me once again, then stomped out of the room.

Mirth was still dancing in the old man's rheumy eyes as he looked at me. "Well now, boy, hope we didn't frighten you."

I shook my head. "Not really. I just—I just—"

"Just what, boy? Spit it out!"

"I needed to ask you a couple of questions."

I could have sworn that the tabby was smirking at me.

"Pardon me, boy," said Thaddeus, "but I need my rest.
There's another full moon tonight. Full enough, at any rate.
What's on yer mind?"

"Mr. Thaddeus, I want to be frank with you. I don't
like the situation I find myself in with regard to your children."

"Neither do I, boy. I'm their father, you know. What
could be worse than that?"

Still wary of the wallboards, I moved closer to the bed
and sat in a decrepit floral armchair. I said, "Sir, my questions will be personal. Very personal. If you feel you don't
want to answer, I'll understand. The only thing I ask is, if
you do answer them, please don't lie to me."

"I won't lie, boy. Hate a liar. Always have. Main reason I like animals better than people is an animal won't lie
to you. Neither will a wolf. Not even a werewolf, though
we're more or less halfbreeds, by a wolf's reckoning. No
sir, boy, if I answer you at all, I guarantee you, 'twon't be
a lie."

I didn't quite know where to begin. He said, "Spit it
out, boy. Don't waste my time and yours mincing words."

I spat it out. "Mr. Thaddeus, you've said you believe
that you're turning into a werewolf, and what I've heard
just now seems to confirm that. Is it true?"

His eyes gleamed feverishly as he thought. Then he
looked me square in the eye and said, "True as any words
that have ever been said."

"Why do you believe this? Have you ever seen a doctor?"

He cackled as if I'd said something hilarious, then replied, "Doctors be damned. Nothing but a bunch of money-
hungry quacks." His eyes seemed to have a reddish cast
to them today. He thought for a minute, then said, "Seen
a witch doctor from Haiti, though. Friendly fellow."

"What did *he* say?"

"Said I should be drinking more blood, then I wouldn't
howl so hoarse nor sprout so much hair. Said it would help

me to see better, too. Thought about it. Seems I'm getting an appetite for blood these days—human, that is, not animal. Couldn't do that to my little friends.''

"You don't eat meat?"

"Vegetarian, boy. Only hankering I got is for human blood." He looked at me speculatively.

I shook off my discomfort and said, "Assuming you're right, when did you first start turning into a werewolf?"

"That's a stupid question, boy. Born that way, I expect. Leastwise, it runs in the family. A family curse." He pointed at the hair tufting out of his ears and upon his head. "See this hair? Gets thicker every day. See these teeth?" He opened is mouth wide and pointed to his incisors. They were indeed large, but no larger, no sharper, than others I'd seen that belonged to perfectly normal human beings.

He clamped his mouth shut and held it that way for a moment, then he said, "Started to really show up about a year or two ago, boy, though I wouldn't expect anyone else to remember. If you'd been around, you'd probably just have ignored it like everybody else. No skin off your backside, after all. But my own skin got to feeling rough and tough, and I'll be damned for a tortoise if I didn't really go to town and start sprouting hair. All over my damned body, just like you see it now! Look!" He opened his pajama shirt to reveal a heavy, furry mat of gray chest hair.

He patted it wistfully and said, "Not a hair on my chest when I was a young man, boy. Not a single hair. Didn't hurt me none with the girls, though. Should have seen the children's mother—hoo, boy, you should have seen the snazzles on that one, and she was head over heels about me, boy, head over heels. Sad day for me when she died."

Suddenly he seemed happy again. He said, "Say, did I ever tell you how I got to be rich?" He waggled a finger at me and said, "My daddy invented a better dog-food. That's how he did it. Made him a fortune. Know how? Found him a secret ingredient, he did. To this day nobody else knows what goes into Thaddeus's dog food. Want to know what it is?"

I nodded.

"Bat guano, boy. What do you say to that?"

I said, "I can see why you like bats so well. . . ."

That brought him up short. "You being smart, boy? Because if you are, I can shut up here and now. I don't have to say another word for the rest of my natural life. You making fun of my bats?" His lower lip stuck out in a pout.

"I just meant—"

"You meant nothing. *Like* is not the word, boy, not the word. The word is respect. I have a great deal of respect for anything that can sleep through an entire day these days. Nuclear war, Chinese in government, people creeping around in shoes with rubber soles—rubber comes from the jungles of South America, you know, boy. This world is a mess. No one like you is going to tell me any different."

"I didn't try," I said mildly.

"What's that?"

"Mr. Thaddeus, you were telling me why you thought you were turning into a werewolf. Remember?"

He looked surprised. "With all the interesting things going on in this world, you still want to hear about that?"

"Yes, sir. I'd like to know."

He smiled widely, showing his large, protruding teeth, and said, "I got a memory sharp as a tack, boy, sharp as a tack. First time I realized the truth was about four years ago. I was laying in this very bed. . . . You know, I've always had a deep admiration for timber wolves. You know timber wolves?"

"Yes, sir," I said, "they're beautiful animals."

He nodded, pleased. "Person could do worse than be born a timber wolf, let me tell you. Anyway, I'd been reading this book about timber wolves when I dozed off. The light was on, this same little reading light." He patted the lamp beside the bed.

"Well, boy, let me tell you, I woke up about three o'clock and it was quiet as anything, and I looked out that very window and saw a fat, full moon sitting right on top of those eucalyptus trees. Well, let me tell you! All of a sudden I knew! I touched my chest, and sure enough, the hair there was twice as thick as it had been when I'd gone to sleep. Boy, the hair on my chest came out gray, just like you see it now." He showed me his bare chest again.

"See these paws on me? Used to be long and skinny. Folks used to pester me to be a concert pianist when I was a boy, said I had the hands for it. Look at them now!"

I had to admit that his hands were clawlike. The nails were long and thick, even though they were clean. There were gray tufts of hair on the backs of his hands, thicker than before. He turned his hands over. There was a half inch of fuzzy gray hair growing out of his palms!

He cackled at the shocked expression on my face. He said, "Think an old man is nuts just because he knows he's turning into a werewolf, do you, young whippersnapper? Well, boy, you'll see. Right along with the rest of them. Not a one of you has seen anything yet! Anyhow, I laid there that night, looking at that full moon, and I felt a growling in my throat that I couldn't hold back. And you know what?"

"What?"

"I loped out there onto that balcony right behind you and I just stood and howled at that full moon until I was just about howled out. And you know what?"

"What?"

"There were timber wolves out there somewhere. They howled, too, right back at me—*with* me, for that matter. Course, I couldn't understand what they were saying back then. Takes a while to make sense of the language. But I can tell you, I knew at that moment what it is to come home and be with family. I can tell you that much, boy. Never had much of a family before then. My son off howling after the girls, my daughter stuck away in those snooty schools. My wife long gone . . . Know what I did, boy?"

"What?"

"Next day I sent someone to find those timber wolves. Found them right across the park, in the city zoo. Know what I did?"

"What?"

"I bought those wolves, boy. Got them to this very day.

In the pens at the back of the estate. Those wolves have turned out to be my very best friends, boy, and no two ways about it.''

"What about your children?"

"Children? We never had children. Never mated with those wolves, boy. Decent man don't mate with family. Nor does a decent wolf.''

"I mean what about Jill and Ta—uh—your human son? What do *they* think about all this?"

"Oh, *those* children. They're after my money, boy. Tried to talk to Jill about it a couple of times. She sent that quack boyfriend of hers out to talk to me. He took pictures of me. Pictures! And measured me all over. Took imprints of my teeth! Never heard the like of it before! Felt like instead of helping me, he was planning to make up a statue of me or something to put on display somewhere. Maybe one of those Believe It or Not places.''

I said, "You mentioned earlier that when the moon was full you get spells. What do you do?"

He shook his head, perplexed. "Can't always remember, boy. Miss Partridge tells me that sometimes I go out and lope around the estate. Says that sometimes I just go out to the wolf pens and chat a spell. She tends to me, makes sure I get in before the sun comes up.''

"The sun? I thought sunlight only hurt vampires."

"Fat lot you know about it, boy. You ever turned into a werewolf? No? Then don't give opinions about things you don't know about. Sunlight hurts the eyes, boy. Makes me weak and meaner than any full moon ever did. Say, boy, couldn't do me a favor, could you?''

"Well, maybe."

"With the moon being full now, I keep getting that hankering for human blood. There's a blood bank up at the El Sangre Hospital. Was up there once when the kids were little to get one of 'em stitched up. Couldn't talk you into running up there and buying a few pints for me, could I?''

"I'm sorry, Mr. Thaddeus, but hospitals don't sell blood like that.''

"Damned nuisance," he said. He got a crafty look on

his face, then said, "Don't suppose they'd miss a few quarts, do you? If you went up there and stole some?"

I decided to humor him. "I'll see what I can do."

CHAPTER
EIGHTEEN

I CALLED ANGELO. "HEY, OLD BUDDY. HOW'S THE TA-males?"

"Hot, amigo. Hey, I don't know what you're doing these days, Weatherby, but you're sure as hell doing it with some bona fide dingbats."

"Dingbats?"

"This Sterling character is worse than I thought he was."

"How so?"

"The guy's taken the meaning of the word quack to new levels. He's created whole new minority groups: the nose-less and chinless."

"Did you dig up anything about sex-change opera-tions?"

"That, too. He's being sued by some guy who thought his dick was being removed. When he got home, he found out he'd only lost his balls. Operation cost him twenty-five grand."

"What about the guy's finances?"

"Poor as dirt. He was a waiter."

"I mean Sterling's."

"Oh! He's poor as dirt, too. He declared bankruptcy about three months ago in order to get some of the lawyers off his back. Last year's batch of lawsuits seem to have wiped him out.''

I said, ''Thanks, buddy. Now for a new subject. What do you know about a gang of bikers who call themselves the Satan's Sadists?''

''Same thing everybody else knows. They're sleaze, pure and simple. They're a ragtag army of small-time thugs who rape grandmothers and kill babies. They'll do anything—anything—for a buck. I've thought about joining them myself a time or two.''

''Know anything about their trafficking in drugs?''

''Does this have something to do with those feds that beat you up and who might even now, at this very moment, have your phone bugged?''

''Relax, Angelo. I checked my phone. The bug must have been at the motel.''

''Then how did they know that you'd been asking questions?''

''Elementary, my dear Angelo. People talk. They must have just put two and two together. Back to the sleazebag bikers. Drug trafficking?''

''Hell, Weatherby, what bike club doesn't?''

''Plenty. There are real live humans who also like motorcycles.''

''Oh, well, yeah, but I mean bikers as in *bikers*.''

I said, ''Angelo, what does a kilo of cocaine go for these days?''

He hummed a bit into the phone, then said, ''Depends on the cut. I'd say the good stuff goes for twenty-five to thirty-five thou per kilo. Maybe even more. Why? You going into business?''

I did some fast calculating. ''Okay, a thousand grams in a kilo. Street price is about a hundred and twenty-five dollars for a gram. That's a profit of—''

''Ninety to a hundred thou per kilo,'' he said. ''Need a partner?''

I said, ''That's a lot of money, and a lot of money buys a lot of protection. I know for a fact that the Satan's Sadists own the sheriff in Desolado. I just keep wondering if they've managed to buy a couple of feds I know, too."

"It's happened before, but not so often as people would like to believe," said Angelo.

"Yeah," I said, "but then what the hell are they so worried about?"

"Well, Weatherby, it's hard to tell these days. You know how the thing works. A syndicate of one kind or another usually controls the trafficking in one area. Someone else tries to move in on them. They use the boys they own in law enforcement and government to wipe out the competition, and the cops and G-men end up looking like plaster saints. Nothing is ever said about the boys still in business. All the cops and feds have done is the legwork for the syndicate. On the other hand, there are a hell of a lot of clean people out there, people who care and who are risking their lives to try to clean things up."

"True," I said. "And they have to put up with the crooked assholes in addition to doing their own work."

"Yeah, I know," said Angelo. "It sort of rankles, doesn't it?"

"If they're crooked, I'd like to take them out," I said.

"And I'd like to see you do it, Weatherby. Let me know what happens. I'll keep my ears open. If I learn anything else, I'll get back to you."

CHAPTER NINETEEN

THE BEST LIBRARY IN TOWN WAS AT THE UNIVERSITY. I drove over there, parked my BMW in the parking lot, and walked through the hallowed halls and into the microfilm room.

There were a dozen other papers in the city beside the *International Inquirer*. I'd decided to take a look at them all.

I came out of the library at ten that night. Taft and Tafoya were the golden boys of the DEA, all right. Scores of busts, and not a hint of dirt in any one of them. Not a blemish.

Still, something was very, very wrong.

I'd already decided to drive back to Desolado the next morning, kick over a few more rocks, and see what skittered out from under them. I knew it would be a little like slitting my wrists and jumping into a pond full of piranhas, but what the hell!

I hadn't been to the office all day. I needed to check my mail, check my answering machine, and replenish my funds from my cash stash in the office safe.

I drove toward the ocean, then turned south on El Agua Drive. Several yachts were anchored far out at sea, their triangles of light the only separation of the blue-black ocean from the blackness of sky. To the west, the city spread out in a more confusing geometry of light that sent out a wide glow, outlining the hills.

The road bore inland a few blocks, and then I was passing the brilliant glitter of the Pacific Funway Amusement Park. It covered the area from the road to the sea. A huge stone monolith towered over an archway entrance protected by a turnstile. A ticket window was cut into the stone wall to the left of the turnstile, and I could see a blur of pink and yellow that must have been the ticket taker.

An enormous red, green, and gold neon sign blazed along the top of the stone wall. Beyond it, the roller coaster was ablaze with light. Cars whizzed along its tracks, and the floating sounds of screams and shouts came from it. Tinier screams pealed through a background of calliope music, and for the few minutes it took me to drive past, the aroma of popcorn wafted pleasantly on the air.

There were a lot of cars in the parking lot. People out to test the glitter and thrills in the gentle night air.

When I got to Quaker, I turned left again, and slowed to a crawl.

The bar next door to my office building was still open, and there were quite a few cars on the street. I cruised along, looking for a parking space.

There was a place right in front of the lobby door!

I slid into it just as a thin man in a cheap gabardine suit walked out of the barroom door with a woman about four feet tall and four feet around. She wore a pink and white lacy, ruffled dress. To the casual observer, the man was taking a pink and white wedding cake for a walk.

After they passed me, I opened the car door. Just as I started to slide out, I saw someone else. In the alley.

A kid, maybe sixteen, seventeen years old. He ventured out of the alley right after the couple passed, but when he saw me, he darted back. I probably wouldn't have noticed him if he hadn't started at the sight of me. He'd had a look of shock on his face.

I'd barely glimpsed him, but the impression had been indelible: dark brown hair, a skeletal body, a gold T-shirt with marijuana leaf design and dark shorts. He'd looked like a feral child, stunned by what he'd found in the city. But that face . . . Somehow, it was vaguely familiar.

I climbed out of the car and sprinted to the alley. The kid was long gone.

I went back to the front door. A faint blue light came from the lobby. I unlocked the glass door, strode across the black and white tile floor, and punched the elevator button.

I rode up to the fourth floor, then stepped out into a hallway that was dark except for one dim bulb in a fixture at the far end. No tiles up here, just ancient hardwood. And something else . . .

There were six offices on this floor, three doors on either side of the hall, each of them with a clouded glass window, all of them vacant except mine and the one that belonged to a bookie who pretended to be a life insurance agent.

No light in any of the windows. Yet I had the certain feeling that someone was either here or just had been. Something was very wrong.

I squinted into the semidarkness, scanning every molding, every corner of the familiar hallway—and then I saw it.

The second door on the right was ever so slightly ajar. At the same instant I saw a thin wash of green light coming through the crack. Suddenly it vanished. It was followed by a gold strip, then red, then green again. I realized it was the neon light from the amusement park, coming through my office window, my barely open office door.

I heard something. I froze, trying to keep my heart from pumping so I could hear. I listened hard enough to break an eardrum. Nothing.

I pulled my gun out of my shoulder holster, stepped silently out of my loafers, then walked silently down the hallway. I was about four feet this side of my office door when I stopped again to listen. A pungent, familiar scent hung in the air. Fresh blood.

And then I heard the noise again. I froze.

I stood like that for an eternal five minutes before my

mind deciphered the sound. It was the slow drip of water coming from the leaky faucet in my bathroom sink. I felt a flood of embarrassment at my stupidity, and at the same time relief.

The wash of red came through the partly opened door and bathed my pant leg, then washed away. I leaned quickly into the office, flipped on the light, then jerked backward, aiming my gun at the door in one smooth motion.

Nothing happened.

I was starting to feel stupid.

Quickly, I stuck my arm into the open doorway again, then drew it back. Nobody shot at me. Nobody threw a knife. Not even so much as a poison dart or an insult.

I reached through the door again, switched the light off, slid through the doorway, and stopped well inside the door. Then I flicked the light on again, my gun aimed and ready.

His back was to me.

He was gazing out the window to the bay—at the huge skeletal cranes on the loading docks, at the carnival glitter of the amusement park beyond the docks and across the water.

Except that he wasn't seeing it.

His head was tilted slightly to one side.

Gun ready, I walked around to face him.

Where his face had been, there was a sodden mass of red pulp. Ivory shards of bone lay in the mush, and the skull had been laid bare in one place. The front of his shirt was a solid mass of red, where the slit in his throat had drained the life from him. Beneath the chair, a pool of blood was still spreading outward. The acrid scent of blood filled the air. His skin was as white now as the blinded eyes of a cave fish.

His skull-and-crossbone rings showed stark against his fingers, their corroded brass showing a slight green tint. The blackened, chipped nails were stark against the thick, blood-drained fingers.

Someone had beaten his face in—with a wrench or something like it—then slit his throat just to make sure.

I went through his pockets. In his hip pocket there was an old tooled-leather wallet. In the wallet there were notes on car parts, a receipt for a new manifold, and my business card, the one I'd given to Uriah Tucker the first time I'd gone to Desolado, the one I'd asked him to give to Tank Thaddeus.

Tank Thaddeus had gotten the message from old man Tucker. He'd found my office.

Now both of them were dead.

CHAPTER
TWENTY

THE BOYS IN BLUE WERE IN AND OUT BY TWO O'CLOCK, taking their fingerprints, their lab evidence, and the body with them.

I'd opened the windows as wide as they'd go. The ammonia I'd used to clean up most of the blood had compounded the slaughterhouse smell, and the cigars and cigarettes of the police hadn't made the smell any better.

The last time I'd seen Tank Thaddeus, he'd been punching my headlights out. Now the medical examiner's attendants had just carried what was left of him out on a white gurney. His remains were en route downtown to be chopped up and analyzed. I wasn't exactly in mourning for him, but I felt bad about how he'd met his demise. In fact, sick as hell.

I wanted to be the one to tell old man Thaddeus.

I closed the window, turned off the lights, locked the door behind me—the lock hadn't been broken and I hadn't been able to explain to the cops how anybody had gotten in—then drove over to the Thaddeus estate. It was half past two when I arrived.

I rang the funereal chimes more than a dozen times before Miss Partridge, looking disgruntled and wearing a dingy terrycloth bathrobe, opened the front door and snarled, "Well?"

"I have to see Mr. Thaddeus right away. It's an emergency."

She glowered at me. "You can't see him tonight."

"Look," I said, "it's his son. He's been murdered."

"Abernathy didn't do it," she said quickly. "He's been out at the zoo all night long."

"What?"

"See there?" She pointed overhead.

An almost full moon hovered just above the western chimneys of the darkened house.

"Hear that?" she asked.

I listened. I could hear dogs howling—or was it wolves? They sounded mournful and far away.

"You can't see him tonight," she repeated defiantly, and tried to slam the door in my face. "I got strict orders."

I stuck my foot in the door. "I want to see him now."

"Don't know why. He didn't do it. Hasn't left the zoo. I've heard him out there all night long."

I said, "Why are you jumping to the conclusion that I think he did it?"

She pointed up toward the moon and said, "Havin' one of his spells. Worse is bound to come to worst someday. But he didn't do it tonight. Not yet."

"I want to see him. Immediately."

She sneered at me but stepped aside. "You just go ahead and push your way in where you're not wanted. You'll get everything you deserve, or my name ain't Mamie Partridge." She turned around and started down the hall, checking to see if I was following her.

I was.

She flipped on the hall light, and suddenly the house was just the same old monster of a house: the cat smells; the bulky, ancient furniture; the same ancient, disgruntled Thaddeuses glaring down from their portraits.

I followed her through a kitchen, where she slid open a drawer in one of the old white cabinets and took out a large flashlight. "The old fool won't let me turn the yard lights on when the moon is full. We'll need this."

I followed her out the back door, down six steps, past a greenhouse with half its panes broken out and a black jungle of plants inside, and through a small forest of ironwoods and eucalyptus. Then she held the flashlight so I could see the corrugated iron fencing that closed in the back side of the estate. Thaddeus had a lot of land here. Enough to start his own game preserve, if he'd wanted to.

As we came out of the trees, she continued to use the flashlight to guide us, though we didn't need it. Moonlight flooded the grounds. The liquid blue of the sky was reflected darkly in the tree shadows. The moon itself seemed pale blue-white. We stepped onto a flagstone walk. We came to a high redwood fence. She opened a gate and I followed her through.

The howling was close now. The animal smell was strong.

We were in a compound of cages. I could see the outlines of several beasts behind the bars, some of them apparently aroused from their sleep by our arrival. A huge cat that looked like a leopard padded back and forth, back and forth.

Miss Partridge smirked. "Don't need to worry about the animals. Only ones out tonight are the wolves."

The howling was closer and closer.

We were past the cages. She then opened an iron gate that led into a small field with trees in it. I said, "But the wolves—"

"They won't hurt *me*!" she said. "Abernathy would have their hides if they did. I'll be right back. You wait here."

The howling diminished into a concerto of conversational snarls, then I heard a thick guttural voice say, "Ah—ah—*arrooo* bothering me again, Miss Partridge?"

"It's that stupid man," she replied. "He insists on seeing you."

There was a snarl, then his voice again: "*Aaaiiyee* don't want to be bothered tonight. Argh! Tell him that!"

"He won't listen. He says it's Ta—uh—it's about your son. He's been killed."

"Ah—ah—*arrooo*," he exclaimed, and I thought there was anguish in it.

She snipped at him. "Oh, Abernathy, what's the harm? He sees you like this, maybe he'll believe you. Most people think you're nuts, you know. Well?"

The gate opened, and she wheeled him through.

The moonlight shone on his face. The man looked baaad, no doubt about it.

His cheeks seemed to have shriveled back from his teeth. They protruded a lot farther than when last I'd seen him. He wore no shirt, and his skinny trunk was covered with a thick mat of gray hair that stuck out wildly. His eyes were much deeper set, red-rimmed, and when he talked there was a growl in the back of his throat that changed his voice to something bestial.

He snarled, "Ar, ar, *arrooo*! Argh! Come to take a look at the old Wolfman, did, *arrooo*, boy? Come to see me have one of my spells?"

I said, "Mr. Thaddeus, sir, I—I'm sorry about the timing. But I wanted you to know that Ta—uh—that your son was killed tonight."

He looked up at the moon. I saw tears run down his face, and he bayed at the moon, long and low and sad. The wolves behind the fence joined him. For a minute there, I felt like baying myself.

Then Thaddeus stopped and looked at me with mournful eyes. "Bound to have happened sooner or later, boy. Ah—ah—*arrooo*!" His face sagged and the predatory teeth protruded even farther.

Miss Partridge said, "Time for you to get to the house now. You're 'bout howled out. Need to get you some rest."

"Narrgh!" he growled, and shook his head.

Miss Partridge looked at me, glaring, and said, "See what you've done? Now he's *really* upset!"

I said, "We should take him to the house and make sure he's all right. That's hard news for anyone, and he's in bad shape already."

Thaddeus snapped at me. "Nnaarrgh!"

"He wants to be alone with his wolves," said Miss Partridge.

"I don't know," I said. "He looks pretty bad."

"Nnaarrgh!" He said it again. Then he grabbed the wheels of his chair and turned it, pushing the gate open as he went back into the compound. Immediately, the howling started again, but mixed into it were little barks and yaps and growls, as if they were comforting him, asking him questions.

I'd had enough.

Miss Partridge led me back to the house. I let her go into the kitchen door, then I found my own way around to my car. I fired her up and hit the gas.

As I drove out through the front gates, I began to pity old man Thaddeus. I had a really queasy feeling. Something was truly wrong with the guy.

And at that moment, I'd have staked damned near anything I had on the possibility that he really was turning into a werewolf.

CHAPTER
TWENTY-ONE

I STOPPED AT AN ALL-NIGHT DINER, DRANK A CUP OF coffee, splashed some cold water on my face, then drove south on the Santa Calzada Freeway. When I came to the Corona del Gardenia exit, I left the freeway and turned east. Jill Thaddeus lived at 905 Bayview Drive.

The condominiums were a series of graystone towers, imposing as medieval fortresses. A high graystone fence surrounded all three of them. A circular driveway passed through opened gates, past well-trimmed lawns and manicured hedges and beneath a row of towering royal palms.

The first crack of sunshine had already slid behind huge gray rain clouds. The sea was a cold pewter. A red-uniformed doorman sat in a glassed-in square beside the front door, napping. It was too early for any other signs of life.

I pulled my BMW up beside the glass, stepped out of the car, then rapped on the pane right beside his head.

His head jerked and his eyes flew open. The instant his brain registered my presence, a prepackaged, frozen smile sealed itself to his face.

I acted unctuous and bossy. I told him I wanted to go to 1703. He acted embarrassed and deferential. He hit the elevator button without bothering to announce me.

The elevator floated upward like a cloud. When it

stopped and the door slid open, I was looking into a small vestibule paneled in blond oak. Two heavy blue upholstered oakwood chairs stood on either side of a polished oak door. I stepped onto the gleaming floor and pushed a buzzer beside the door.

I waited about two minutes, then I pushed it again and held it.

As she opened the door, Jill Thaddeus was brushing a strand of hair out of her sleepy eyes, holding a green silk robe partially around her. She squeezed her eyes shut, then opened them, trying to come awake. "Who—" She saw me. She tried to shove me back as I stepped inside. "You!" she said in astonishment. "How dare you come here like this!"

"Miss Thaddeus, I—"

"Hush! Worth's here. I—I—"

A man's voice came from another room. It was well modulated, with that trace of phony English accent that some pretentious Americans affect in order to be thought blue-blooded. He said, "Who is it, dear?"

"Nobody." To me, she hissed, "Get out of here."

"Nobody?" he said. "I heard the bell ring. What are you doing up?"

She was shoving at me for all she was worth, but it was too late. He came through the bedroom door, pulling a white silk robe around him. His silver hair was only slightly disheveled.

He looked at me with a haughty curiosity. I looked back.

His tan was deep and golden. He appeared to be in his early fifties. The silver hair, disheveled though it was, had an expensive cut and was snowy white at the temples. He was lean and athletic, in damned good shape.

He smiled at me. Small, thin lips, a pinched smile that surprised me by showing two baby dimples in his gaunt, tanned cheeks. His pale gray eyes stayed as cold as the water at the bottom of the Arctic Sea. There was a mixture of disdain and contempt in his voice as he said, "And who have we here?" He looked haughtily at Jill and said, "Perhaps you'd care to introduce us?" To me, he said, "I'm

Dr. Worthington Sterling, the lady's fiancé. And who might you be?''

"I might be in a lot of trouble."

He frowned in a way that managed to lift his eyebrows and depress them all at the same time. "I beg your pardon?''

I stuck out my hand. He ignored it. "I'm Artie Weatherby," I explained. "I've been doing some work for your fiancée. I'm glad you're here."

His nostrils flared in a partial sneer. Jill, wide-eyed, said, "You are?''

"Miss Thaddeus, I apologize for bothering you like this, but something's happened to your brother."

Her eyes filled with anguish and fear. She touched the engagement ring, toyed with it nervously.

"Maybe you should sit down," I added.

Sterling was suddenly very solicitous. He went to her and put his arm around her. She went slightly stiff. He led her toward a dark gold sofa. "Here, darling, right over here.''

I followed them into the room. When they were sitting side by side on the sofa, I folded into a chair across from them and said, "Miss Thaddeus, I'm sorry. There's no easy way to say this. Tank was killed last night. Murdered.''

She looked only slightly more stunned. In a raw whisper, she said, "I knew, I just knew. Something—something awful just—just *had* to come out of—''

Sterling squeezed her hand. "Bloody hell! How did it happen?''

I said, "I found him last night. His body was in my office.''

"In *your* office?'' Sterling looked at Jill with an obviously feigned warmth. "It seems that I'm in the dark about something here.''

Jill looked down at the chocolate-brown carpet.

I said, "I'm a private detective, Doctor. Your fiancée hired me to find her brother."

Warmly, lovingly, he said, "Well, I'm sure she must have thought she had good reason to deceive me about it."

She started to weep, her shoulders heaving slightly as she tried to stifle the sobs.

"There, there," he said, putting his arms around her, "he wasn't much of a brother to you anyway, was he?"

She sniffled and shook her head. I didn't know if she was agreeing or not.

I said, "Well, I'm intruding. I just wanted to let you know."

Sterling turned again to me. "Do the police have any idea who did it?"

"Not many people crack a case that fast."

He gave me that little up-down frown again. "No witnesses?"

"Maybe a spider or two."

"He was killed *in* your office, you say?"

"No doubt about it. But I have no idea how he got in."

"You'd spoken to him?"

"I tried a few days ago. He didn't much want to talk."

Jill still sat there crying silently. Sterling had taken his arm away from her and was totally focused on me now. He asked, "What did he say?"

"About what?"

"About anything. What he was doing, where he was, what he was up to."

Jill's head shot up and she gave Sterling a dark look that I couldn't interpret, then she buried her head in her hands. "You all right?" I asked. "Shall I call a doctor?"

She shook her head no. Sterling looked at me snidely and said, "You seem to forget that *I'm* a doctor. I'll take care of her." He reached over and patted her knee, then returned his interest to me. "What did Tank say to you?"

"Do you believe in nonverbal communication?"

He frowned. "You're changing the subject."

"Not really. You see, I didn't have much of a conversation with Tank. He was too busy helping those freaking Neanderthals punch my headlights out. But his NVC told me a lot.

"He said the coke's better out in the desert, and easier to get." I watched Sterling carefully. No reaction.

I said, "He said that he'd a helluva lot rather be stoked out on good coke and riding a Harley out there with the lizards and cacti than sitting in an office reading *The Wall Street Journal*. He said his nose had crystallized and his veins were on the way and his brain so numbed out that nothing much mattered anymore. And, oh, yeah, in real words he said he didn't want anything to do with Jill or her schemes."

Sterling leaned over to Jill, then cupped her tear-streaked face in his slender hands. He peered deep into her still-dazed eyes and said, "What else have you been keeping from me?"

Her face went hard for just an instant, and then her shoulders slumped and she mumbled, "I—I don't know what he was talking about!"

Sterling looked at me defiantly. "There. You see? The man had become a coke addict. I told Jill. He was keeping dangerous company. I tried to get Jill to leave him alone. She wouldn't listen. And now he's dead, beyond harm and beyond harming others. Jill's lucky she didn't end up the same way, mixing into his business and sending you to spy on those coke-ridden fiends!"

Jill gave him a withering stare, then looked at me.

Sterling said hastily, "At any rate, if you were hired to find him, I suppose your work is done. We won't detain you any longer."

"I—I—" Jill began.

"Has the man been paid, darling?"

"We'll worry about that later," I said.

"Oh, no," he insisted, "we'll get the matter cleared up now so there won't be any loose ends dangling. Jill won't be requiring your services anymore. I have no idea why she retained you in the first place, when she has me."

"I'll send you a bill," I said.

"Will five thousand be enough?" asked Jill.

I started to shake my head and stand, but something in

Sterling's face, something in the way he was looking at Jill, made me settle in again.

He said to her, "Write him out a check, dear." She did as she was told, then handed the check to me.

Sterling said, "Payment in full for services rendered. I assume that will suffice?"

"More than adequately," I said, standing up.

"Then I assume that ends your arrangement with my fiancée. You won't be needing to see her anymore. Forgive me, Mr. Weatherby, but I am a most possessive man, and old-fashioned enough to want to handle my future wife's problems without some stranger interfering."

He looked at her and smiled. She tried to smile back.

"Well," I sighed, "I guess I can tell when I'm not wanted. Miss Thaddeus, if you change your mind, you have my phone number."

"She won't," Sterling said, too shortly. "*We* won't be needing your help anymore. Ever. Good day, Mr. Weatherby. Thanks for coming."

CHAPTER
TWENTY-TWO

THE PHONE WAS RINGING AS I WALKED IN MY FRONT door. It was Angelo.

"Good early morning, boy wonder," I said.

"Hey, Weatherby. Just got the word from the cop shop on the DOA in the office of one Arthur Weatherby of 221 Quaker Street. Got any good juicy quotes for the story I'm writing?"

"Nah. I've already been famous. Now I just want to be rich. Did you get the medical examiner's report yet?"

"Sí, señor."

"And?"

"Do you believe in werewolves?"

I almost dropped the phone. "Huh? What the hell *is* this?"

"Seriously. They found out something strange about Tank Thaddeus when they performed the autopsy—"

"What? That he turned into a werewolf because the moon was full and ripped out his own throat and clawed off his own face?"

"Hey, old man, what's bugging you? The cause of death was verified. Multiple blows to the face compounded by a severed carotid artery. But guess what they found, amigo. When they tested the blood."

"Cocaine?"

"Nope."

"Meth?"

"Well, maybe some. But that's not what I'm driving at. Guess again."

"What's in it for me if I'm right?"

"Knowledge."

"Tell me."

"They found out the guy had *porphyria*! Isn't that weird?"

"Porphyria? Isn't that when your skin flakes and itches and you get red splotches? And you get all heartbroken?"

"Hell, no, that's psoriasis. Thaddeus had porphyria."

"Mind translating?"

"Not at all. I'm looking at a stack of papers I got from the medical examiner."

His voice turned into a monotone as he read to me. "Porphyria is a rare disease of the blood that is most often hereditary. It is caused by a defective substance called *heme*. Heme is a component of the blood. One of the most telling symptoms of the disease is sudden growth of excessive hair. Skin damage may also occur, making the victim appear to have shriveling skin. Muscles around the mouth may draw up, making the victim's teeth appear more prominent. Other symptoms of this extremely rare disease are a painful photosensitivity, or aversion to sunlight; irritability; disorientation; and other neurological disturbances, such as hallucinations. When the human body chemistry changes with the advent of the full moon, the victim of porphyria may indeed believe that he/she is transforming into another physical form. Experts believe that the many cases of porphyria during the Middle Ages led to the myths of vampires and werewolves. The disease, fortunately, is treatable today, even though there are several varieties of porphyria. The most common treatment is the periodic injection of a blood compound that replaces the faulty heme in the blood. . . ."

I was speechless.

"Weatherby? You still there?"

"Yeah. Yeah, Angelo, I'm still here."

"What did I say? Did I do something wrong?"

"No."

"Then talk to me!"

"I'll talk to you later, Angelo. Something's come up."

CHAPTER
TWENTY-THREE

As Alice used to say, curiouser and curiouser.

Old man Thaddeus *was* turning into a werewolf—except that he wasn't.

When I'd recovered from the initial shock, I called the Thaddeus mansion.

Miss Partridge answered the phone. She snarled at me and explained that the old man was sound asleep, and then she slammed down the receiver.

I spent about five minutes mulling things over. I decided to drive back out to the desert and see if anybody there wanted to play.

Desolado was still sleepy and sun-drenched. I wheeled my BMW off the parched pavement of the highway. My tires crackled against the gravel. The pink neon sign above the doorway to Sandy's Tavern blinked wearily off and on and off and on.

In the store next door, the windows had been shrouded over with green vinyl shades. A square of cardboard had been tacked crookedly to the padlocked door. Someone had spray-painted one black word on it: CLOSED. Dust had already settled on the porch, the window ledges, and the gas pumps.

I opened the tavern door and stepped into the same mildewed darkness with the same combination of musty and acrid odors. The same configuration of drinkers sat near the end of the bar, transfixed by the television set. They were watching a morning soap. Nobody had bothered to feed the jukebox. It sat there, glowing its primary colors, grandfather to the beer signs behind the bar, awaiting its chance to howl.

Mabel recognized me. She climbed off the three-legged stool she'd been sitting on behind the bar, waddled over to me, and said, "What'll it be?"

"Shot and a beer. And send one to my friend down there, too."

She glanced around at the drinkers, then looked back at me and asked, "Ya mean Mick?"

"Yeah."

She poured my shot and beer, poured another for Mick, swept my twenty up off the bar, rang most of it up, gave me a few dollars change, then slammed the boilermaker in front of Mick. She said something to him, swinging her meaty thumb in my direction. He grinned and nodded. I motioned for him to join me.

He slid down to my end of the bar. "Nice to see you again," I said. He gave me a toothless grin, tossed off his shot, followed it with beer, and slid the empty glasses toward Mabel.

I said, "I was on my way to the border. Wanted to pick up a few things at the store. Know when it's going to open up again?"

Mabel laid her palm on the bar, face up. Mick gestured toward the empty glasses. *One Thousand and One Ways to Extort a Private Eye*, Chapter Two.

I pushed my own shot and beer over in front of Mick, then deposited the change from the twenty into Mabel's fat little hand.

Mabel spoke first, since Mick was busy with the booze. "Man that owned it died. Ain't goin' to be openin' for a while."

"What happened?" I tried to sound politely curious. "Accident?"

"Died a natural death. Eatin' at them damned pistachio nuts all the time. Too much salt on them. Salt's bad for the heart. Had a heart attack—"

"A heart attack?"

Her eyes narrowed. Her puffy mouth twisted up, and she said, "You questionin' my word? 'Cause if you are—"

"It'll be no trouble a'tall to call old Bryce Canyon," I finished for her.

"Bryce Canyon?" she asked. "What you want to call him for? Matter of fact, he's the one what told me about it. Got it from the horse's mouth himself."

"Anybody but Canyon see the body?"

That seemed to make Mabel mad. She snorted, "Whadda ya think we are out here, anyways? Bunch o' ghouls like you city folks? Why in hell'd I want ta see the body?"

Mick wiped foam off his mouth and said sagely, "Next o' kin'd be the only onsh ta worry 'bout that. If he'da had next o' kin. Didn't."

"When's the funeral?" I asked them.

"Yestidday," said Mick. "Old Uriah Tucker is already shtuck in the ground. Ashes ta—" He hiccuped, then said, "County planted 'im."

I turned to Mabel. "You seen Tank Thaddeus around lately?"

She opened her palm again. I took out the old eel-skin, extracted a ten, and laid it in. The hand folded around it like crocodile jaws. She said, "He was in here a few days ago. On his way out to the landing strip."

"Landing strip?"

Mick mumbled, 'So much damn buzzin' these days, gettin' sos a man can't shleep out in the open—"

Sharper than I'd intended, I asked, "You get a lot of airplanes landing here?"

"Not all that many," Mabel said. The topic didn't seem to bother her. "Mostly Mexes from across the border. The only one comes from anyplace you'd be interested in is that flesh-pink Cessna, one that belongs to that highfalutin doctor friend o' Nails McNulty's."

"Doctor? You said doctor?" I was digging furiously in

the old eel-skin. I whipped out two twenties, laid one in each person's hand, and said, "What's the doctor's name?"

Mabel snorted and said, "Never got it. But he was a tall, skinny fellow with silver hair. Thought he was a big deal. Came in here once with them bikers, tried to tell me I was too fat. Rude bastard. Said I ought to drive into the city—that he could make me look good as new. Never got his name, though. Didn't want it."

Mick said, "Feller's got him a shnazzy car, too."

"A car? He drives out sometimes?"

"Sometimes."

"What kind of car?"

"New, fancy job."

"What color?"

"Pinkish. Same color as the airplane."

"Look," I said excitedly, "I really appreciate this. Can you tell me one more thing?"

Mabel's hand flew open. Mick nodded sadly at his empty glasses.

But before I could take the last few bills from my wallet, the air outside was ripped through with a deafening thunder that sent both Mabel and Mick scampering back to the far end of the bar.

Chapter
Twenty-four

THE METALLIC THUNDER WAS GROWING LOUDER. Motorcycles were screeching up to a halt; engines were being revved to maximum capacity; people were shouting orders and greetings over the din. Nails McNulty crashed through the front door. The bikers outside played with their accelerators, revving their engines, then letting them wind down, performing the evil orchestration that every bad-assed bike club in the world uses as its formal announcement of arrival.

Nails stood inside the door, holding it open with a booted foot. He was looking around the barroom now. His arms were crossed like Attila the Hun's. His eyes found me and stopped. He fingered the chain at his belt.

The noise outside was dying off. Other bikers were tromping through the door, too, now.

And they were looking at me. Every last one of them. And stopping as soon as they saw me.

The other people in the bar were fading off into dim corners. Mabel swung back over to me and said, "Buster, if you tell 'em I've been talkin' to you, I'll kill you myself!" She nodded piously, then went back to her perch.

Nails stomped up to me and growled, "You asshole. Thought you could come right back out here and nobody

124

would notice you? Thought we were that stupid?'' He jerked a greasy thumb toward an anemic-looking drunk cowering at the end of the bar. ''Jimmy there called us as soon as you got here.''

I remembered seeing the skinny man get up right after I'd sat down at the bar. He'd gone to the back. I'd thought he'd gone to the bathroom.

''We've got snitches everywhere. Everywhere! We own this town.'' Nails' large, pale eyes stared at me with all the personality of a dead fish.

A man with a bulbous nose and close-set eyes said, ''We was dumb not to kill 'im when he give us the chance. I says now that we doesn't talk. We kills 'im.'' I recognized the voice.

''Shaddup, Stinky,'' said Nails.

Another biker stepped forward. He was short and square, with dark black hair. His enormous beard and mustache almost obliterated his face. With red hair and a pirate's hat, he'd have looked like Yosemite Sam. He wore faded Levi's pants and a Levi's vest, covered over by patches declaring that he was a member of the Satan's Sadists. He growled, ''Yeah, Nails, whatcha gonna do? Let 'im go again?''

''Shaddup, Snake,'' said Nails. Then he reached forward and grabbed the front of my shirt. He tried to lift me off the bar stool. His six-foot frame strained, and the muscles popped out in his arms; the cords popped out in his neck. He couldn't move me. I'd gone limp, giving him pure dead weight. He backed off and said, ''You asshole.''

Two other bikers had moved to block me off from the door. Both of them were swinging lengths of heavy chain, twirling them like slingshots. One of them stepped forward. ''Need some help, Nails?''

''Shaddup, Lester.''

A brown-haired biker who appeared to be about eighteen stood to one side. He was cleaning his nails with a huge knife. He said, ''Do somethin', Nails. Want me to cut his nuts out?''

Nails' lantern jaw clenched. His fish eyes bugged.

"Shaddup, Grimy. All of you, just shaddup! *I'm* the president here, and *I* say what we do!"

"Then *say* what we do," two of them grumbled at the same time.

"Shaddup, shaddup," said Nails.

He grabbed me. I saw it coming and twisted to one side, so he grabbed a handful of my shirt. It tore as I writhed away, leaving him with a handful of white cotton. I was off the bar stool, spinning around to face them, my weight on the balls of my feet and my hands in a karate parry. I felt heady. My adrenaline was pumping, and I was ready to take on all these grease-brained sadists at the same time.

Nails got a nasty, spiteful look on his face. He opened his hammy fist and dropped the white cloth to the floor. Then he reached into his belt sheath and pulled out a hideously serrated knife with a bone-white handle and a ten-inch blade. One of the bikers chuckled and said, "Go for it, Nails. Chop the bastard up."

"Shaddup, Jonesie," Nails said. "Shaddup all of you, just shaddup!"

He lunged at me.

I ducked, bringing my arm up in a swift block. I felt his arm crunch as I made contact, saw his knife go flying through the air. He grabbed his broken arm with his other hand and went dancing off toward the far end of the room, wailing in agony. "Oww! The bastid broke it!"

Lester the Molester came forward next, a sick grin showing the stumps of his rotting teeth. He swung the length of chain above his head. It kept him just enough off balance so that when I whirled around and gave him a side snap kick to the legs, he caved to the floor. Another snap kick to the side of his head and pinwheels blazed in his eyes. His head sagged as his eyes went blank. He was over and out.

The others were in a frenzy now. They had a cocaine high going. Their adrenaline surged. They were practically snorting at the nostrils and foaming at the mouth. Snake, Greasy, and Stinky came at me, one of them with a lead pipe in his hand, one holding a baseball bat, one wielding a knife. My fist connected with a beer-fattened gut. My foot snap-kicked into someone's leg and I heard it crack. My arm came up in a block. An arm snapped back and the lead pipe went flying. I caught my breath. I was staring straight into a pair of red drug-numbed eyes, and then my hand connected to the side of his head in a swift chop. Another body sagged to the floor.

The boy with the baseball bat had a fringe of hair around a bald spot and a face like an obscene friar's. He clenched the bat up and aimed for my head. I ducked just in time. The bat connected with the skull of the dark side's answer to Yosemite Sam, and the little feller sank to the floor, too. I ducked into the man who'd held the bat, then spun around. The flat of my foot connected with his rib cage. The snapping sounded like a run on a marimba.

My gun was in my ankle holster, but I didn't go for it. Frankly, I was having fun. It had been a long time since I'd gotten my exercise, and it felt good to know that everything still worked. These boys weren't pros. Nothing at all like the VC, just a good morning's workout. They were soft from too much dope and too much booze. The toughest acts they'd committed lately were playing pool and ripping off grandmothers. They were used to scaring people to death with their reputations, the monstrous ways they looked—and all that motorcycle noise.

But they were in a frenzy now, and coked out besides. And most of them had grown fat and bloated on violence. Yeah, watch it, Weatherby. These grease-impacted monsters would kill you if you gave them the chance.

Stinky had recovered enough to make another attack. Jonesie was on my back, just hanging on. Nails reeled forward, one arm hanging limp at his side. In his good hand he had the bone-handled knife. He lunged again, trying to stick it into my throat. I grabbed his arm, whipped him forward, and slammed him into Stinky, who was just getting ready to bring the baseball bat down on my head. Stinky staggered around, found his footing, yelled, "You mothah—" and brought the bat down just as I spun. It slammed straight across Jonesie's spine. He lost his hold and tumbled off my back.

I was panting now. As soon as one of them dropped off, another took his place.

I was tired of playing. I wanted my gun in my hand.

I stepped back from them, tried to reach for my ankle holster, but Snake dived at me. His teeth clamped rabidly around four of my fingers. I howled. Stinky was coming back at me from the other side. I dropped him with another side snap kick. He fell to the floor. At the same time, I curled my bleeding fingers up inside Snake's mad-dog mouth, and dug into the nerves at the base of his tongue. His jaw sagged as his bite slackened. At that I ripped up and out to tear his jaw out of socket. His howl turned into a scream and one more biker was out of the game.

I was in rare form, fine-tuned by righteous rage. I was wheeling about, fists up, karate blocks and punches flying. And then there was a break in the madhouse choreography and I grabbed my .38 and spun around to aim it—but all the bodies were gone. Nothing to the north, south, east, or west but air. Just air.

Blinking hard and swallowing, I ticked around like the hand on a time bomb, covering every part of the room in steps. Mabel was hunched down at the front of the bar, beneath the television set. There were two bleary-eyed drunks barricaded beneath a turned-over table in the corner of the room. The jukebox sat there, still waiting for its chance to blare, and the bikers were gone, out the front door.

I sagged onto a bar stool just as the evil orchestration of the revving engines began, signaling their departure.

The front door opened, amplifying the noise. *She* walked in.

She moved like cream flowing out of a pitcher. Her face was an even deeper golden color than it had been a few days ago. Her eyes were serene and peaceful—and un-drugged.

She glanced contemptuously at Mabel, then walked straight across the floor and sat down beside me. She was chewing gum, and she rolled it over to one side of her mouth and said, "Didn't learn yet, huh?"

"I've learned one thing, doll—"

"Doll?" Her golden eyebrows shot up in arches and her nose wrinkled in distaste. "Did you actually call me doll? Who do you think you are, Mike Hammer?"

That embarrassed me. Mostly because I *had* picked it up from some shamus on TV. "You're way too good for these lice," I said. "Come back to the city with me. No matter what happened to bring you this low, I'll help you get a fresh start."

"Like what?" She looked amused.

"Well, I could use a good secretary."

"I don't type," She *was* laughing, but not exactly at me.

"I'm not leaving you here. Some heavy action is going to start up around here very soon, and I'm not going to let you get caught up in it."

"Action?" Her eyes became slits. They turned as cold as a rattlesnake's. "Such as?" she hissed.

The front door flew open before I could answer her. Nails stood there, a sawed-off shotgun aimed square at my guts.

Crystal hissed, "Quick! Grab me and put me in front of you."

"What?" I was looking at the shotgun, barely able to concentrate on what she was saying.

"Grab me! Here!" She all but did it for me, throwing herself between me and the shotgun. I instinctively tightened my arm as she slid it around her shoulders and pressed herself back at me.

It must have looked like the real thing from where Nails stood, because he said, "Let her go, asshole. This is between us men."

She whispered urgently up at me, "They need me. I'm the quality-control expert for their dope. They've got a shipment coming in a few hours, and they're afraid the Mexicans are going to rip them off. They won't want me to get hurt. Come on, idiot, make it look like I'm your hostage.''

I cleared my throat. "I—I'm holding the girl—"

"Let her go, asshole, or I'll shoot you both."

"He won't," Crystal whispered. Out loud, she said. "Don't, Nails. He's holding a gun in my back. He'll kill me."

"You stupid cow," he exclaimed. "Why'd you come in here? I told you I was going to kill him."

I said, "I'm coming through that door. If you shoot, you'll kill the girl."

"I'm not a girl, you idiot. I'm a woman!" She stomped down on the insole of my foot. I winced. Nails said, "That's the way, Crystal, get away from him."

Loudly, she said, "I can't, Nails. He'll shoot me. Let us go. It's not worth it. We can get him later. I'll get away somehow. You know me."

He thought for a minute, then nodded. "Yeah. You'll get away. And as soon as you do, you'd better scoot right back here."

"I'll be all right, Nails," she said reassuringly as she moved me out the door.

Nails stepped in behind us. As we sidled past the gang sitting astride their bikes, he shouted, "Let them go. He's holding her hostage!"

The bikers snarled and growled, but they let us pass. I managed to get my gun back in my hand as I opened the passenger side of the car and shoved her in. "Ouch!" she said. "Let's not get so damned realistic!"

I waved the gun around conspicuously, then slid in under the steering wheel. I said to her, "Now what?"

"Now we drive away. Leaving Nails and his playmates behind. Unless you want to stay here."

"So you *are* coming back with me?"

"No. Let's get out of here."

"Where are we going?"

"To the city, fool. Anywhere. Just hit the gas before they change their minds!"

I gunned the engine, shifted gears, and spun gravel as I

headed for the highway. In mere seconds we were tooling down the highway and toward the freeway entrance.

I stayed silent for a while, then turned to her and said, "What is it that ties you to those sleazeballs?"

"This is not the time to explain."

I pulled the car onto a shoulder of the road and stopped. "Look, you don't ever act stoned, but who can tell. If you have a drug habit, I'll get you into a good rehab center I know. I did some time there myself, dried out from the booze. It took a long time to get my life together after I came back from the war—"

"I don't use drugs."

Cynically, I said, "Oh, I see. You just deal them. So that you can get rich by causing brain damage to half the human race, not to mention all the birth defects and other misery—"

"I don't need a lecture," she said. She started to open the car door.

I pushed the button that automatically locked all the doors. "What do you think you're doing?" she asked.

"You're going back to the city with me."

"I'm not. I can't."

"Why?"

"You'd never understand."

"Try me."

"I can't. Let me out. I have to get back."

"You're strung out."

"I'm not." She was looking at me in astonishment. "Why do you keep saying that?"

"You're the pearl cast before all those swine, and I'm not going to let you go back there."

Her mouth fell open at that, and a little flush came to her cheeks. She laughed out loud. "So you're going to reform me?"

"If I can."

"You're nuts! What do you have, a Don Quixote complex?"

"Maybe."

"Well, sir—"

"Weatherby. My name is Artie Weatherby."

"You *are* nuts!" She looked at her wristwatch and said, "Man, I have to go."

"What's the rush?"

"I'll level with you. I have a coke buy at four P.M. Exactly one hour from now. Two of the biggest sellers from Mexico are flying up from La Bahía. We're giving them ten Mercedes Benzes, two Rolls-Royces, three Cadillacs, and two Jags—not to mention a cool half million in cash. They're bringing us kilo upon kilo of nice, clean coke."

"So that really is what all of you do out here?"

"It is. Open the car door. I have to go."

"And all the bikers are involved in it?"

"Yes."

"How many of them?"

"What difference does it make? Look, I don't have time for all this."

"How many?"

"Oh, damn it, let's see. There's Nails and Stinky, and Greasy and Jonesie, Snake and Lester the Molester. And there was Tank."

"What is this, Snow and the Seven Dwarfs? What part do you play, Snow White?"

Her face froze into a horrified expression. She gasped. "How—what do you know?"

"About what?"

"Are you working for the cops or something?"

"No."

She said, "It wouldn't matter if you were. We own the sheriff here, and we have the top boys in federal law enforcement paid off, too."

I thought about Taft and Tafoya.

A sixteen-wheeler with an oil tank on the back was rolling down the slope, going toward Desolado.

Suddenly she had a knife in my ribs. "Open my door, please."

I opened it.

She slid quickly across the seat and out the door, and

then, before I could get out my own door, she was in the middle of the highway, arms waving, shouting, "Help! Help! Please stop and help me! He was—" But the rest of what she said was lost in the sound of the truck's air brakes as it skidded to a halt.

She was up and into the cab before the driver knew what had hit him. I started to follow her, but the driver's head pivoted and he glared at me and gestured with fists doubled up. She was shaking her head at him and pointing in the direction of Desolado.

I decided it was time for me to butt out.

The driver shifted gears and wheeled his rig down the freeway toward Desolado. And the girl of my dreams was gone, gone, gone.

CHAPTER
TWENTY-FIVE

ANOTHER DAY THROUGH THE LOOKING GLASS AND INTO that universe where everything is exactly ass-backward from what you expect it to be . . .

I needed to rest, to clear my brain, to think things through. . . .

When I turned on the lights in my house and chased out the ghosts again, I opened a bottle of mineral water. I went out to the patio, where I could look past the black swirls and lashes of trees hanging on the sides of the canyon, and down to the mist of city lights. I swigged the water to try to get rid of the gunmetal taste at the back of my throat, the taste that had been there ever since the girl of my dreams had run away with a trucker.

The mineral water didn't help.

There was something about Crystal's being a part of the slit-throated, morally numbed out, humanly decayed world of cocaine trafficking that put a different light on my own world. A light that showed all the corruption in the tiny cracks of existence, all the moral disease that lay just beneath the polished veneer of illusion that most of us think is reality. I'd felt like that a few times in my life. The last time had been right after I'd gotten home from Nam, when I was working my way through law school on the G.I. bill, and working nights to fill up the slack in my budget. I'd wanted the law degree to complement the wife and 2.5 children that I was planning to secure. And then I'd found out my girl had been letting my best friend jump her bones while I was away at school.

I got up and tossed the mineral water bottle in the trash, then went into the bathroom. I took a shower to wash away the dust, shaved, and then brushed my teeth—hard. Out, out, damned spot.

After slipping into some comfortable clothes, I went into the kitchen.

I turned on the oven, then opened the freezer and took out a large package of frozen king crab legs. I put them into a shallow pan, then stuck them into the oven to thaw. Not the best way, but the quickest.

I took out fresh mushrooms, two ripe tomatoes, a bell pepper, some celery, a half dozen long-stemmed green onions, and chopped them all into large chunks. Then I peeled two garlic cloves and minced them, almost to mush. I put some brown rice into the rice cooker, then heated my wok and tossed in a pat of butter and swirled the minced garlic in it. Then I added salt, brown sugar, and a pinch of curry, stirring it all the while. The sweet, pungent, curried fragrance woke up my appetite. When the butter had completely melted, I scoured the inside of the wok with some rich red wine. It burst up in a puff of fragrant steam. My stomach growled.

I took the crab legs out of the oven. They were thawed through, but cooked not at all. One by one I tossed them into the wok. When they were all in, I stir-fried them, tossing them around in the thin, steamy wine-butter syrup until the red and white of the legs were golden brown and the insides just barely cooked all the way through. I took them out, heaped them back into the pan, then stuck them into the oven for a few minutes while I stir-fried the vegetables. I took them out while they were still crisp, then I put a bed of brown rice on a large plate, topped it with the vegetables, then laid on the crab legs.

I put the platter on a tray, poured myself a cup of hot

green tea, used my real silverware—a wedding gift I'd never returned—then took it all into the living room.

It was time again for my favorite television show.

The theme song was playing. Bert Baxter, teeth agleam and dimples dimpling, was introducing the panelists. Betty and Veronica were flashing their long legs. I cracked a crab leg and bit into the succulent meat while the pretaped audience howled and clapped and roared.

Baxter held up a perfectly manicured hand. The applause faded. "And now," he said, "our first contestant."

The camera panned over and locked onto the contestant's face.

My mouth dropped open. My arm jerked up in an involuntary reaction, and tea sloshed out of the cup and into the rice.

It was him! The kid who'd been in the alley the night I'd found Tank's body in my office. I peered at the TV. No doubt about it. The same skeletal body, even the same T-shirt and shorts. And that same, vaguely familiar face. Why did he seem familiar to me?

What difference did it make? It was him!

I was on my feet and hurling toward the bedroom even as Baxter was saying, "And now, judges, here's your report on your contestant—"

I slid into a pair of sneakers, grabbed my wallet and car keys, and was already on my way out the door, crab legs and TV forgotten, when I heard Baxter's dim voice saying, "You all know the rules—"

I was halfway to the TV studio before Betty and Veronica had another chance to flex their pects.

CHAPTER
TWENTY-SIX

THE GUARD AT THE BACK DOOR OF THE TV STATION was elderly and underpaid. His palsied hand wrapped around the fifty I held out to him like it was manna from heaven, and he opened the door.

I stepped into a huge, warehouselike room with open rafters. There were flats stored, backdrops for various TV shows. I stepped over cables as thick as my arm and past rows of klieg lights of various sizes and heights, almost all of them painted industrial gray. There were boxes and crates and piles and stacks of electronic equipment that I didn't recognize, and there were several cameras, some high up on dollies and others on tripods.

I could hear Baxter's nontelevised but still amplified voice saying, "An excellent guess, ladies and gentlemen, an excellent guess!" I peered onstage, careful to remain behind the backdrop of the set.

I was looking squarely at the boy. He sat hunched up in the contestant's chair, with Betty and Veronica keeping vigil on either side of him. He looked twitchy and stunned.

Baxter said, "Our young contestant's line was . . . co-caine!"

Canned whooping, canned howling . . .

Baxter's familiar spiel continued: "In just a moment

137

we'll award our prizes. But first, this word from one of our sponsors—'' The camera man was giving him the ''cut'' sign. Baxter relaxed and looked his age for a minute. Betty and Veronica dropped their frozen smiles and helped the kid up out of the contestant's chair.

He jerked away from them, managed to pull himself together into a stance that oddly enough had some dignity to it. They backed away from him and he headed toward me, toward the back door.

Funny. I'd never until then wondered what happened to the contestants *after* the show. . . .

I hid behind a cluster of klieg lights and watched him walk through the vast, high-raftered room. He looked small now, alone. He shoved open the back door and went out into the night.

I dashed after the kid. He was in the alley, leaning up against the wall. I stepped over to him. He looked at me blankly for a moment, then turned away. He started walking down the alley. He was definitely stoned.

I let him walk a little ways, then I caught up with him and touched his shoulder. He stopped.

"Hey, remember me?" I asked.

He froze. I stepped around in front of him. "So how did you like being on TV?"

His eyes were too wilted to make contact with mine. "I saw you once before," I said. "Do you remember me?"

"No man, no man, no way, I don't remember nothing, never, never. Got me, man? Nothing."

I said, "A couple of nights ago you were standing in an alley beside my office building on Quaker. I drove up in an ice-gray BMW. Do you remember me now?"

He had a flat, dead fear in his eyes. He stepped back against the building, faltered, caught himself, then turned back again and tried to run.

With two swift steps, I caught up to him. I grabbed his shoulder. He only came up to my own shoulders, and he was so skinny that I could almost hear his bones chattering together as he stopped short. He looked up at me with wild eyes and said, "Let me go, man. Got to get me some blow."

"Yeah, kid, I know. You've already got all the trouble you can handle just staying on top of that habit. Look, I'm not here to hurt you. But a man was found dead in my office the night I saw you in the alley. The way you jumped and ran, I thought you might know something."

He tried to pull away from me.

"Where do you live?" I asked. "Maybe we could go there. I can drop you off."

He shook his head back and forth and shivered.

I said, "I need to talk to you. Want something to eat?"

"I need some snow, man. Like, right now."

He wasn't exactly in the same class as a junkie on a jones, but anybody who maintains that cocaine isn't habit-forming is either as stupid as the dullest, flattest rock in the ground, or else they're dealing the stuff. His body was processing out the poison he'd put into it, and he needed more to get well. More still if he wanted to get high again. Which he most likely would as soon as he got well.

"I can get you some coke," I said.

He wrapped his arms around himself and, through chattering teeth, asked, "Where?"

"Come on," I said. "I have a friend who tends bar in a joint where some of the Satan's Sadists hang out. They're the biggest dealers in the city. He'll score for us."

The kid was too sick to be grateful. I grabbed his shoulder and steered him toward the car.

Five minutes later we pulled up in front of the White Dolphin Bar & Grill over on Dock Street. It was the sort of dive where nobody paid any attention to the sore losers caving the winners' heads in with cue sticks in the back alley, much less to ID's. I took the kid in with me.

The joint was packed. There were several factions of local bikers hogging the pool tables, while other, more timid souls waited for them to get through cheating one another. I steered the kid past the pool tables, pimps, and pushers. We made it up to the bar.

Joey Vegitalis had once been a prizefighter. His brains

had become predictably scrambled, and his other options had predictably disappeared when he'd been shoved out the back door by the crime syndicate that had owned him. He slopped his bar rag toward us, looked around to see who was watching, then said, "How do, Weatherby. You ever find that guy in the picture? One you was asking me 'bout, one I seen down in Desolado at the pool tournament?"

"I did, thanks, Joey. He was right where you'd seen him. You've got a sharp eye, pal."

"Only for you. You know how to keep yer yap shut." He eyed the kid beside me and said, "Where'd you get the sick little runt?"

"He needs some coke, Joey. Somebody's got him strung out."

He shrugged his massive shoulders and said, "Don't seem like you to score dope for a kid, but if that's what you want, you come to the right place. Must be two dozen street dealers in here right this minute."

I pulled out the old eel-skin and extracted a C note. Joey said, "Gram'll cost ya more than that. Goin' for a bill an' a quarter these days, if ya want anything halfway clean."

"Get me some good stuff," the kid pleaded.

I bowed to greed and need and extracted another bill. The kid tweaked at his nose while Joey took the money and rumbled down the bar. He motioned for a grease-stained Neanderthal with a cue stick to join him. They put their heads together. In under five seconds, the biker had reached inside his leather vest, pulled something out, and dropped my money into his pocket. Joey came back up the bar and dropped a tiny cellophane packet filled with white powder into my hand. He said, "If it ain't good, you know who to see."

I said, "Thanks, Joey. Keep the change as a down payment on the next favor I might need."

As soon as we were back inside the car, the kid had the packet open and was snorting the coke up through a plastic straw he'd grabbed in the bar. I backed out of the parking place. "You got a place to stay?"

He shook his head.

I said, "You're welcome to stay with me for a few days, if you like."

He was mellowing out a little. He said, "If I stay with you and we do anything, you have to give me money."

I reached over and slapped him, not hard, just enough to sting his face. "Watch your mouth, boy," I said. "I'm the old-fashioned kind. I'm old enough to remember when being called a trick was an insult. I offered you a place to stay. I may look old and moldy to you, but I've managed to live a few years without turning into the kind of slime you've evidently been associating with."

He got a surly look on his face. I said, "You ever think about cleaning up? Getting off the dope?"

He was a little high now, and he went through one of those rapid transformations of mood that cokeheads are famous for. He grinned and said, "Sure. I can quit any time I want to."

"Why don't you want to?"

He lost the momentary rush and looked sulky again. "Don't know."

"You got a family?"

"A stepmother. My dad's dead."

We were passing a drive-in restaurant. I pulled in and said, "You want a sandwich? Hamburger?"

"No."

I ordered him a burger and order of fries—better than nothing and maybe something he'd eat, anyway—then asked him, "You live with your stepmother?"

"No."

"Why not?" He was hunched up against the door, trying to fold in on himself.

He said, "She doesn't want me. I cramp her style."

"How so?"

"Aw, hell, man, she's got too many boyfriends, doesn't want them to know she has a kid as old as me, even if I am just her stepkid. She sent me to live with these creepy friends her and her doctor boyfriend have."

"Doctor?" Suddenly I remembered where I'd first seen this boy again.

"Yeah, man, she has this weird boyfriend who's a doctor. He didn't want me around."

"What were you doing at my office building that night?"

"I followed them."

"Followed who?"

"Marnie. My stepmom. And her boyfriend."

"Marnie?" It almost caught in my throat and didn't come out.

"Yeah. What's the big deal? Marnie Evans. She's my stepmom—anyway, she's the one who married my dad about a year ago, after my real mom died."

"What happened to your dad?"

"He started drinking a lot after he married Marnie. He ran his car off a ramp on Lemon Boulevard one night. Marnie got me and all his money. All she wanted was the money."

I suddenly realized why the kid had looked vaguely familiar to me. There was more than a slight resemblance to the oil portrait of the old man in Marnie's living room. I said, "And you aren't living with your stepmom's friends anymore?"

"Hell, man, they didn't want me either. All they were interested in was dealing coke. I couldn't stand them. I left. I've been working the streets for a few months now."

"Working how?"

He gave me a surly look.

"Doesn't she even give you money to live on?" I asked.

He gave me a harsh little laugh.

The hamburger and fries arrived. I handed them to him and said, "Eat."

"I'm not hungry."

"Humor a senior citizen. Eat anyway."

His mouth turned up in a faint grin and he took a small bite out of the burger. I said, "How long since you ate?"

"I don't know."

"How old are you?"

"Nineteen."

"Try again. I'm not the cops, you know."

"Fifteen," he said, nibbling at the bun.

"How long you been strung out?"

"I'm not strung out."

"Have it your way. How long have you been using coke?"

"Since my dad married *her*. She has it there all the time. I just started helping myself."

"What were you doing at my office building? Tell me the truth. A man was killed, and it's damned important that I find out why."

"I didn't know anything about that."

"What happened? Why were you there?"

"I ripped off a car and followed Marnie. I was going to rip off her apartment, get her jewelry and some of the cash she always had." He'd laid the hamburger on the dash and the words just started tumbling out. "I was really broke, and these guys I'd been getting my coke from were mad at me—they'd been fronting me dope and they said I owed them eight hundred dollars. If I didn't pay them, they were going to beat me up. I couldn't figure out where to get the money. I called Marnie. She just laughed and called me a spoiled little brat, told me to figure it out for myself. So I got mad at her and decided to rob her. I still had a key to the apartment. But I wanted to make sure she wouldn't catch me. I ripped off this car that had been sitting in the park, and I went over to where I used to live and waited for her and Sterling to come out."

"Sterling?"

"Dr. Sterling. Her boyfriend. He did some surgery on her when she was still married to my dad. They belonged to the same country club. I used to go there, too, play tennis, swim. . . ." He sounded like an old man remembering a lifetime long past. "They used to—to go to bed together when she was still married to my dad. I told her to stop, or I was going to tell, but she just laughed—told me to go ahead, maybe it would give the old goat a heart attack. My dad was pretty old to have a kid as young as me." He had a sad, sad look on his face. He was studying his hands as he talked, turning them over and then back, looking at them carefully, giving himself something to do to help keep the pain away.

I said, "So you followed them to my office. What happened? Did they stop anywhere on the way? Was anybody else with them?"

"They didn't stop. Nobody else was with them."

"Well, what did they do?"

"Nothing. They just went in."

"Wait a minute. How long were they there? I mean, how long before I arrived did they get there?"

He shrugged his shoulders. "Not very long."

"How did they get in?"

"I don't know. They just opened the front door and walked into the lobby, then hit the elevator button."

"They had keys?"

"Yeah, I guess so. Yeah, I remember, they opened the door with keys."

Red alert. So that was why little Marnie had been so hot for my bod, why she'd tried so hard to pour her plum champagne down my throat. She'd wanted me out of my clothes—out of it *all* long enough to be able to get an impression of my keys.

But what had they wanted in my office? And if they *had* killed Tank Thaddeus, why had they done it there?

I said, "Think carefully. Try to remember everything. How long were they inside? How did they act? Did they say anything you could hear?"

"I'm not sure about how long. I parked my car around the block, then went back through the alley. They couldn't have been in there more than a few minutes, because I'd just started to turn the corner when they came flying out, and they both looked real white and scared. They climbed into a car—not the one Sterling usually drives but an old black car—and took off fast. I'd just started to turn around to go get my own car when you drove up and pulled into the same parking space they'd just left. I was scared. I think it was the way Marnie and Sterling acted. So I hid there. I didn't want them to see me. And then I'd just started out of the alley again when you drove up. I thought at first that you might be a cop. Are you?''

''I told you, I'm not a cop. I'm a P.I., as in private investigator.''

His grin was fully developed this time. ''Like on TV?''

''Not exactly. My gun only carries five cartridges. I can't dodge bullets, and I only get laid every other month or so. My name's Weatherby. Artie Weatherby.''

''That's a weird name.''

''What's yours?''

''Brian. Brian Evans.''

''Look, Brian, I have things to do, places to go, cases to solve. You want to go to my house and watch TV?''

''Nah. I'll just get out here.''

''I don't think I'll let you do that,'' I said.

''You can't stop me.''

''Wrong. I can call the real cops. You're a minor.''

He looked stricken. ''Don't do that. Marnie told me that if I got in trouble with the cops, she'd put me in reform school. Don't call them.''

I said, ''Look, I used to be a juicer. I have a couple of friends. One of them used to be a medic with my unit in Nam—''

''You fought in Vietnam?''

''Right. And so did my buddy, Dr. Straussler. He and his wife run a clinic now. They started it to help vets who were having problems with booze and dope. I spent a few months there. It's not a bad place. How'd you like to go see them?''

''Nah.''

''Why not?''

''I don't have any money.''

''Marnie does. I'll get some of it for you.''

He looked at me with disbelief and said, ''How?''

I said, ''Extortion. I'm good at that. Want to go meet Sam and Gerry Straussler?''

''Nah.''

''Why not?''

''What's the use?''

I said, "Look, Brian. Accept some words of wisdom from Weatherby. There are a lot of us in this world who don't fit the mold—for better or for worse. Maybe we get some raw breaks, like out parents die, or maybe our parents are so screwed up themselves they don't even know we exist. That doesn't mean that something's wrong with us. It just means that we got some bad breaks. But sometimes that's good, Brian, because we have to make it by ourselves. And that makes us strong. And sometimes, if we get strong enough, we can even make the rest of it right from time to time."

"It doesn't matter. Nobody cares if I live or die."

"Don't you care?"

"Nah."

"Come off it. You care, Brian. And that's what matters. What say you just spend the night with the Strausslers and listen to what they have to say. Then if you don't like it, I'll get you an apartment of your own tomorrow."

He looked at me with disbelief again and said, "You'd do that?"

"I would. Whatta ya say?"

He shrugged his shoulders and said, "Well, yeah, I guess so. Why not?"

I backed out of the drive-in and we were on our way.

CHAPTER
TWENTY-SEVEN

SUDDENLY ALL ROADS WERE LEADING TO STERLING AND his Romanesque nose. I checked my watch as soon as I'd dropped the kid off at the clinic. It was seven minutes past eleven. Time for me to indulge in a shamus's favorite pastime: breaking and entering.

I sped south on El Agua, slowed down for the speed traps in Bay City, cruised past the gas stations and motels, and then drove past the neon-lit shabbiness of Bay City's hobo row.

I turned east on Embustero Street and looped back up and toward the exclusive business district of Brevity Hills. The phone book had given Dr. Worthington Sterling's business address as 975 Riata Drive.

I cruised past huge squares of window, well lit to show mannequins in mink, sable, and ermine stoles, to show diamond rings and five-hundred-dollar scarves and mink-lined toilet seats and diamond-studded collars for poodles. After six or eight blocks of this Thorstein Veblen nightmare, I was in the residential area, passing huge iron fences with sentries posted at iron gates and opulent rooftops peeking up from faraway trees.

I passed a medical center set in grounds that looked like a movie set for *Gone With the Wind*, and then I came around the corner, and dead ahead of me was Sterling's clinic. It was a large white building with a rust and brown Mexican tiled roof. It had once been someone's estate. There was a wide paved parking lot in front of it and enough shrubs and date palms to make it look lush and exclusive. Lights of various colors had been set back in the heavy shrubbery, helping to illuminate the grounds. There was one streetlight above the parking lot. The windows were all dark except for the reception area. There were dim night-lights inside. From the car I could see a waiting room full of paisley chairs, mirrors, and potted palms.

I drove around and parked on a side street. Then I cut through the back of Sterling's grounds. When I'd gotten to the back of the clinic, I checked the back door. Child's play.

I went around to the front just to check things again. Nobody there. I noticed the small gold-plated sign beside the front door: DR. WORTHINGTON STERLING, PLASTIC SURGERY.

I went around to the back again, took out my set of lock picks, and had the door open in under a minute.

My flashlight showed a polished gray floor in a hallway. The place smelled of antiseptic. I floated through, opening first one door, then another. The rooms were cold from the air conditioning, but colder still from something else—something ephemeral that permeated the place. I padded through rooms with white-shrouded examination tables, with scalpels agleam in faintly illuminated sterilizing machines. There were rooms full of white canvas laundry bags and folded gurneys with gleaming chrome frames.

I struck gold on the last door on the left. It was locked. I had it open in under half a minute. I swept my flashlight through the room.

The large teakwood desk on my right held only a sleek pen and pencil set, a gold sculpture of a woman's torso, and an ink blotter. On the wall to my left was a full-length anatomy chart of a woman. There were two paisley armchairs against the wall and another one across from the desk—obviously for the comfort of the patient being shilled into the fold. On the walls were hundreds of photographs, before and afters, of chin lifts, face lifts, breast lifts, thigh lifts, nose jobs, breast augmentation—any adjustment that could be made to the human form was depicted there.

And the entire wall to my left was covered with wooden filing cabinets.

It didn't take me long. Every file was in order. I went to the *M* cabinet first.

McNulty, Bruce.

I pulled the file out, then sat down on the edge of the teakwood desk and used my flashlight to read. Nothing remarkable there. Bruce, a.k.a. Bunny, had first been to see Sterling eighteen months ago. Her sex-change surgery had been performed almost a year ago to the day. I put the file back and went to the *E*s.

Evans, Marnie Patricia.

Over the past two years, she'd had a face lift, a buttocks lift, breast augmentation, and a chemical peel. According to the records, over twenty thousand dollars' worth of plastic surgery. Sterling had used the surgical terms for the operations, but I found a dictionary of medical terminology on his desk and translated in nothing flat.

I left Marnie's file on the desk, then went back to the cabinets.

I opened the *T* file. I wanted some info on Jill Thaddeus.

I thumbed through the manila folders, looking for *Thaddeus*.

I found it.

The folder was thick, thick, thick. I pulled it out, took it over to the desk, and turned my flashlight on it before I noticed that the initial after *Thaddeus* was *A*, not *J*. I opened the folder.

The name inked neatly across the top of the inside cover was Thaddeus, Abernathy II. A file on the old man! *That* not only knocked my socks off; it set some bells to ringing, too—most of them alarms!

What the hell was Sterling doing with a file on the old man?

According to both Jill *and* her father, Sterling had never treated the old man, never so much as laid a stethoscope against his chest. Why, then, was this file here?

I opened it carefully. Photographs spilled out onto the desk: eight-by-ten glossies, blow-ups, right and left profile, full-on shots, pictures of the top of the old man's head, close-ups of his ears, his nose, his chin—every part of his face and neck. Inked onto the margins of the photos were cubic-centimeter measurements of every part of Thaddeus' face, neck, cranium, jaw—even his upper torso. I picked them up, looked through them carefully, then laid them back inside the folder and took out the sheafs of papers accompanying them.

These were detailed diagrams of the old man's physical build, the length of his upper arms, his lower arms, each finger, both hands, his torso, his pelvis, thigh, calves, feet. There were also lists of his clothing sizes and preferences and page after page of details about his personal habits.

Yet there were no records of any surgery. Not even so much as a mole removed. And no record, either, of any other medical treatment.

What the—?

I left the file on the desk and went back to the file cabinets. I pulled Jill's file.

She hadn't lied to me about consulting Sterling about breast surgery, anyway. Nor had any surgery been performed on her. The papers were dull reading, until I got to the last page in the file.

One of those alarms rang again!

It was a financial statement of the old man's worth—right down to the property taxes due for that year on his estate. What the hell did it all mean?

Sterling was putting Jill together for her money—or for the money she'd have if the old man didn't disinherit her. That much was apparent. But then that much had been apparent since I'd learned that Sterling was in deep financial trouble.

No point in keeping Jill's file out. I started to put it back, when for some reason I glanced at the next file in the cabinet.

Tucker, U.

Serendipity doo-da! I whipped it out and shined my light inside it.

Tucker, Uriah H.

This file was thick, too. I spread it open. It was also filled with photographs, almost identical to the ones that Sterling had taken of Thaddeus. The only ones that were noticeably different were some nude shots. Old man Tucker was glaring into the camera. His scrotum was shriveled up and his hands were poised as if he wanted to hide his penis. He was glaring at the camera. There were shots of his nose, ears, ankles, toes, every part of his body. And inked into the margins of the pictures were cubic-centimeter measurements, just as there had been on the pictures of Abernathy Thaddeus.

Funny I hadn't noticed the resemblance before.

I opened the Thaddeus file again and took out the profile and front-on shots. I laid them side by side with Tucker's. Take the thick gray hair off Thaddeus' head, shave his neck, and you had a dead ringer for old man Tucker—with only a few minor modifications.

I studied the photos.

Lower Tucker's ears a little, raise the eyebrows, maybe thicken the tip of the nose. They were the same height, almost the same weight. . . .

I'd stumbled onto a remodeling job in progress. Except that I happened to know that old man Tucker was dead.

I put Tucker's photos back into the file, then noticed for the first time the *Deceased* that had been penciled lightly across the front of the manila folder.

Now I knew how old man Tucker had planned to get his new Ferrari and his trip to the Bahamas. He'd been planning to light his *cee-gars* with twenty-dollar bills belonging to Abernathy Thaddeus.

Sterling was proving to be a very evil Pygmalion, indeed!

My little gray cells were telling me that Sterling had

bribed Tucker to act as stand-in for Thaddeus—at least until Sterling could figure out how to get his hands on the Thaddeus family fortune.

It would have to have worked something like this: Thaddeus planned to disinherit Jill if she married Sterling. Sterling didn't want Jill; he wanted the money. Enter the Scheme. Sterling would find someone to take Thaddeus' place long enough to convince any interested parties that Thaddeus had changed his mind about the disinheritance. Long enough to cover forgeries of any necessary papers. And then Tucker could be disposed of, one way or another, and Sterling would have the girl *and* the money. Until he disposed of the girl . . .

He'd most likely been traveling out to the desert for a long time. It seemed obvious that he had something to do with the cocaine traffic. Elementary. He'd seen Tucker, and the Scheme had been born.

But why, then, was Tucker dead? If my deductions were correct, why wasn't Thaddeus dead and Tucker ensconced in the Thaddeus mansion?

Why was old man Tucker dead? And, as long as we were on the subject, why was Tank Thaddeus dead?

Suddenly I remembered Tank's words: ". . . I don't want nothin' to do with my sister. Tell her I don't want nothin' to do with her scheme. Tell her that that bigshot boyfriend of hers is—" And then Bunny had interrupted him.

Her scheme? Was this, indeed, Jill's scheme, as well as Sterling's? Maybe Tank had stumbled into it, and they'd killed him to keep him from blowing the whistle. He must have known *something*.

Then Jill *was* in on Sterling's game to get rid of her father. And what had they been planning to do with Thaddeus *père*? Hide him somewhere? Most likely kill him. Yet Jill didn't seem the type to kill her own father for his money. Did she? Stranger things had happened, yet somehow I couldn't see her going that far.

But why had she been so damned curious about Tank's activities in the desert? Did she want to know if Tank was

wise to them? And why in the hell had she hired me behind
Sterling's back? There was a lot going on here that I still
didn't understand.

I looked at my watch. One A.M.

I'd been here a lot longer than I'd planned. Still—there
might be even more info in those files.

Swiftly, I rummaged through them, looking for thick
files, as thick as those on Thaddeus and Tucker. I struck
paydirt on about the seventh one: Graves, R.

I opened it up and took out the photos. Staring up at me
was another man who might have been a triplet for Tucker
and Thaddeus. Eureka!

I scooped up the three files, added Marnie's as an after-
thought, and crept out the door, down the antiseptic hallway, and out the back exit.

CHAPTER
TWENTY-EIGHT

ACCORDING TO THE FILE, ROBERT GRAVES LIVED AT
9916 East Seventeenth Street. He was employed as a jan-
itor at the Brevity Hills Athletic Club. It took me only two
phone calls to ascertain that he was still alive, still employed in the same place, and that, yes, Dr. Worthington
Sterling was indeed a member of the club.

So Sterling's scheme was far from finished. He'd already
found a replacement for Tucker.

What to do next? I slept until a semicivilized hour, then
drove over to the Thaddeus estate. The old man and I had
a lot to discuss.

Miss Partridge wasn't glad to see me. When she opened
the door, she gave me her now familiar withering look and
snarled, "Well?" The broken veins were brighter against
the violet and white today. She kept brushing at a strand
of the gray-flecked red hair. It kept bouncing back like
wire.

Politely, I said, "Good morning, Miss Partridge. I need
to see Mr. Thaddeus."

"Don't s'pose I could stop you if I wanted to," she
muttered, then motioned for me to follow her down the
dark hallway.

Abernathy Thaddeus was in the plant-filled parlor this morning. He seemed cheerful and chipper.

"Hello there, hello there, boy. Come to see my bats, have you?" The tabby had been asleep in his lap. She opened her eyes and scowled at me. I noticed that there was an opened bottle of wine on the little table beside him, and a couple of glasses beside that, one half full.

"Good morning, sir. Sorry to bother you so early."

"No bother at all. Just engaging in a little morning libation. A bad habit Miss Partridge introduced me to. Hard to live alone, boy. Tell you the truth, I'll be glad when I finally get moved down to the zoo. Want a glass of wine?"

I started to decline, but he interrupted me. "Wine builds up the blood, boy, builds it right up." He started to pour a glassful, but the bottle was empty. His thick gray eyebrows dropped down in a frown. He snorted, "Now what in the Cain and Abel—? *Miss Partridge!*" He reached up and tugged at a little cord. A bell jangled far away.

"That damned woman. Pardon my manners, boy. Have yourself a seat. Right over there." He motioned me toward a settee that was set back in a small jungle of rubber trees and ferns.

I started toward it when he said, "Hsst!" He squinted and grabbed a rock from the bowlful on his tray. He hurled the rock toward the settee. Something small with sharp teeth darted from beneath it. I got a glimpse of another long tail as it vanished back into the plants. I walked over and sat in a chair beside the brown light filtering through the closed drapes.

Miss Partridge stomped into the room.

Thaddeus growled, "Try to serve a guest a friendly glass of wine and what happens around here? None left, I see. None at all. And a full bottle here not half an hour ago. And just what happened to it, I ask you."

Miss Partridge scowled at him. The tabby opened her eyes and gave him an identical look. Miss Partridge said, "You know good and well what happened. You drank every last drop!"

Thaddeus scowled back. "I did not."

"Did too!"

"Did not!"

"Did too!"

The cat gave one of her malevolent smiles and made a little noise that was halfway between a belch and a purr.

Thaddeus said, "Well, by damn and thunder, get us some more, Miss Partridge! No sense in standing here arguing all day. What's done is done. Get us some more, I say. I'd like to serve Mr.—uh—what did you say your name was, boy?"

"Weatherby. Artie Weatherby. I really don't want any wine, sir."

"Nonsense. Every red-blooded American needs wine. Miss Partridge! Get us a fresh bottle!"

"I can't," she slurred.

"Why not? Drink too much to walk?"

"We're out," she replied, really scowling.

"Out?" He was getting mad now. "How can we be out? Jill told me that she'd brought you two bottles of that Châteâu Diderot as a gift. You holding out on us, Miss Partridge?"

She snorted. "Drink all of your own, blame me for it, then take mine. That's just like you, you selfish weasel."

"Bring us some wine, Miss Partridge! Or—"

She snorted again and stomped out the door.

Suddenly, Thaddeus grabbed up more pebbles and hurled them at the jungle of plants, yelling, 'Hsst! Hsst! Scat! Damn. That woman's right. Insects *aren't* the only things'll take over if you let 'em. No sirree!" He threw another handful of pebbles at the corner of the room where the plants were thickest. The leaves rustled as something scampered back into them. He said, "I'm getting damned tired of things." He scowled down at the tabby and said, "Supposed to be a cat, aren't you? Why don't you *do* anything?"

The cat looked at him contemptuously.

He said, "Jill tried to warn me. Told me they'd try to take over if I let them live here. Said they weren't the same as other animals. There! Hsst! Scat!'' He threw another rock, then muttered, ''Damn rats, anyway!''

''Rats?'' I was horrified. ''You mean those noises—that scratching—'' I'd thought hamsters, maybe even mice. But rats? I thought about the scratching and scraping, thought about how many rats must live inside these walls, inside this house.

Thaddeus nodded, scratched his furry head, and said, ''That's right, boy. Rats. First animals I ever got so's I didn't like, but I'll tell you, boy, they're more like humans than animals. No respect for the rights of others. I can tell you that. Shouldn't have taken 'em in, but what's a man to do when something poor and homeless comes along? Damn, they put one over on me.

''Trouble with the little devils is, they can't keep their hands off their women. All that rustling in the walls, then next thing you know, here comes a whole new crop of baby rats. No manners, no upbringing. Just left to gnaw away at the innards of the house, roam wherever they've a mind to.''

''But how can you live in a house that's full of rats?'' I'd pulled my feet up onto the rungs of my chair.

Miss Partridge shoved through the door. She was swinging a full bottle of wine. She strode over to Thaddeus, slammed the bottle onto the table without saying a word, grabbed up the empty one, and stomped back out the door.

Thaddeus cackled. ''Now, there's an uppity woman if ever I knew one. Mighta married her at one time, if she'da had me. Wasn't interested.'' He opened the bottle, refilled his glass, then poured a second glassful for me. He ignored my protestations, rolling his wheelchair over to me and handing me the glass. ''Drink up, boy. Wine's good for the blood!''

I took the glass, just to humor him, and placed it on a table beside me. He rolled back to his own table.

There was a quick rustling in the plants. Thaddeus shouted, ''Hsst!'' and grabbed up a rock. The cat, unnoticed by Thaddeus, slid off his lap and onto the table.

As Thaddeus threw the rock, the cat looked at me, gave me a sly look of complicity, then turned to the old man's wineglass and started lapping furiously at the wine.

Thaddeus reached for his wineglass. He saw the cat there, still lapping away, and said, "Now, what in the Cain and Abel—"

The cat's back arched. She let out a chilling scream. She twisted, jerked, and pivoted around to face Thaddeus. Flecks of foam were coming from her mouth. She screamed again, the sound almost human, then fell to the carpet. She went rigid, then gave one massive shudder.

Thaddeus, his mouth open in horror, sat looking back and forth from the cat to the glass of wine. I jumped up, grabbed the glass, and smelled it.

Bitter almonds: the old, familiar scent of cyanide.

I said it out loud.

"Cyanide? Like in rat poison?"

I nodded.

"But who would want to poison my cat?"

"It wasn't meant for the cat, Mr. Thaddeus. Isn't that one of the bottles of wine that Jill brought for Miss Partridge?"

"Yes, but what—"

"Wouldn't it be wise to assume that the poison was meant for Miss Partridge? Mr. Thaddeus, your daughter brought the wine. You opened it. Had the cork been tampered with?"

He scratched his mane of hair. "Seems like it *was* a bit easier than usual to open, boy."

Seriously, I said, "Mr. Thaddeus, we need to talk."

He frowned. "Thought that was what we were doing, boy. Seemed like it, anyway."

"Mr. Thaddeus, call Miss Partridge. She should be here, too."

He looked down at the cat sprawled on the carpet, then back at me. There were tears in his eyes. "Loved that cat," he said. "She was like one of my own children. I'll say that for her. Just like one of my own children." Suddenly feisty again, he pulled at the cord. The bell jingled in the other part of the house, and at the same time he shouted, "Miss Partridge. *Miss Partridge*!"

She swaggered through the door, saw the dead cat, put the back of her hand to her mouth, and took a long step backward.

Thaddeus said, "See there? Dead, ain't she? Killed by *your* wine, Miss Partridge."

"My—my wine?" She could barely talk.

"Not exactly," I said. "Someone put rat poison in the wine. Cyanide."

"Rat poison?"

"You been bringing rat poison into my house, woman? Have you?"

"Yes!" she screamed. "I'm sick and tired of the crawly little things. Sick of them being underfoot, sick of them being in the walls, scratching around all the time. I wanted to kill them, yes, yes, yes!"

Thaddeus was nodding piously.

She'd turned the faucets on and everything was all pouring out now. "I *hated* the little things! Rat droppings everywhere. In the flour, in the sugar—everywhere I went. And everywhere I looked, there they were, spying on me." Her eyes became slits of pure hatred. "Oh, yes, Mr. Thaddeus, I bought the rat poison. I was going to kill every one. But I didn't put the poison in the wine." Suddenly her eyes went wide with realization. "I—I was going to drink that wine myself, as soon as I'd finished the other bottle."

"Other bottle?" I asked.

She gave me an impertinent look. "The other bottle."

"Do you mean the other bottle that Jill brought to you?"

She gave me that look reserved for very slow learners. "What else?"

"Did you drink any of it yet?"

"Most of it."

"And you're still alive?" She just stared at me. "W-well," I stammered, "I mean—"

"Going to kill my rats," Thaddeus said. "*Killed* my cat! Blast you, woman."

She screamed, "I did not put the rat poison in the wine! It's your fault, you old coot, for letting that damned cat get drunk every day of its worthless life!"

"Hsst! What's this? Speak up, Miss Partridge. If you have anything to say about me, just speak up."

She was sulking now. "You're impossible."

"Impossible, am I? I've been going through hell here, turning into a werewolf and all—"

"Ha!" she said in contempt.

"How would you like to be turning into a werewolf, Miss Partridge? Answer me that." He turned his rage on me. "Or *you*, for that matter, you impertinent young whippersnapper. Huh? How would you like to be a werewolf?"

"Sir," I said, "that's one of the things I need to talk to you about."

"What? You trying to tell me that you're a werewolf, too? Don't look like it to me. That boy of mine, now that was a different story. Started sprouting all that hair. I knew that the family curse was catchin' up to him, too. Better the way it is, I'd say."

I said, "Sir, an autopsy was performed on your son."

He scowled. "Found out he was turnin' into an animal, they most likely planned to package him up and sell him at the closest supermarket, if you ask me."

"Sir, they discovered that your son had a very rare disease."

"Disease? Fat lot you know about it, boy. It's a curse, is what it is. A family curse or I'll eat my own hat."

"Sir," I said as gently as I could, "have you ever heard of a rare blood disease known as porphyria?"

"Had one known as diarrhea once."

Patiently, I said, "Mr. Thaddeus, porphyria is a disease that affects a person's heme—"

"Don't have any of that stuff. Don't much want none, either."

"Sir, heme is a substance in your blood. If it's defective, it can cause porphyria. The potential for the disease can be inherited. It may have been in your family for centuries.

Who knows? That's probably where you got the idea that it was a family curse. Tank was probably in the early stages, and you have all these symptoms—"

Miss Partridge said, "Sounds like some newfangled ideas you youngsters have come up with. Never heard nothing about it in my day."

I said, "Are you a registered nurse?"

"Nurse of veterinary medicine. That's why Thaddeus here hired me."

"I see. Well, Mr. Thaddeus, you *do* have most of the symptoms of the disease."

"Symptoms?" asked Thaddeus. "You mean it's something that wolves can get?"

"Wolves?" He'd thrown me again.

"Because you see, boy, I'm more wolf than human at this point, and damned proud of it, too." He stroked the thick gray hair on the back of his hand.

"Mr. Thaddeus, hirsutism is one of the symptoms of the disease."

"Her-soot-ism? Speak up, boy, looks like things are gettin' so bad that I can't understand your words anymore."

"Hirsutism simply means an excessive growth of hair," I said, "like your own. Like Ta—uh—like your son had."

He scratched at the hair on his head, then at the tufts around his neck, then at his robe-clad chest. "One man's cake is another's poison." He glanced down at the cat, then looked back at me. "I might seem hairy to you, boy, but to the wolves, I'm downright bald."

I forged ahead. "Mr. Thaddeus, another symptom of the disease is photosensitivity. An excessive sensitivity to light."

He blinked twice and looked at me like he was starting to listen.

"Another symptom is neurological disturbances. These might come in the form of paranoia or depression, maybe hallucinations. Sir, it's a fact that when the moon is full, a person's chemistry changes slightly. Many people who are already sick are deeply affected by a full moon. Even the slight changes in your body chemistry might cue off the hallucinations.''

"Hogwash. That's easy enough for you to say, but what about the blood?''

"Blood?''

"Damned tootin'. I'm sitting here right now so damned thirsty that I could almost tear out your jugular vein.''

My hand flew to the spot he was staring at on my neck. ''Uh, yes, sir, that fits, too. Your body isn't manufacturing a component in your blood that you desperately need. Your craving for blood might easily be explained as your body's signal that something's very wrong. In fact, the key treatment for porphyria is the injection of blood.''

That got him excited. "You mean to say you could actually get me blood when I wanted it? Just for the askin'?''

I nodded.

"Well, if that doesn't beat the bank!'' "Might be worth lookin' into. Tell you the truth, I'm gettin' so's I dread the full moon comin' on, these days. Might be gettin' too old to sit on my haunches and bay at the moon.'' He licked his lips and said, ''Them doctors would give me shots of blood, you say?''

"Not whiskey shots of blood,'' I said. "Hypodermic shots.''

"A man has to be satisfied with what he can get. How can I get in touch with these folks that give out blood?''

I handed him a folded paper. "Here's a doctor's name and phone number. He specializes in porphyria cases. It's a very rare disease. He'll be happy to hear from you and happy to treat you.''

Thaddeus took the paper and handed it to Miss Partridge. "Probably just another damned quack,'' she exclaimed.

"Miss Partridge, he's the best doctor in the city,'' I said. "He'll help. Promise me that you'll call him for an appointment. He might even be good enough to come to the house, considering Mr. Thaddeus's age.''

Sulkily, she nodded. I said, "Now back to the wine."

"Don't think I want any more, thanks," Thaddeus confessed.

Miss Partridge said, "He wasn't asking you to drink it, you old coot." Her head flew around and she stared at me defiantly. "I know what you're thinking. I didn't put rat poison in that wine."

"I didn't think you had. In fact, Miss Partridge, I believe the poison was put in long before the wine was ever delivered to this house, and I think it was intended for you."

She gasped. "You think *Jill* did it?"

"Not Jill. Her boyfriend, Dr. Worthington Sterling."

Briefly, I told them about finding the files. I explained about Jill's hiring me and about Tank's refusing to participate in the scheme. That perked him up a bit. And then I told them why I thought Sterling might want to kill Miss Partridge. "You see," I said to her, "you're the last fly in the ointment. The only one left—besides Jill, of course, and Sterling evidently controls her—who'd be certain to notice that Mr. Thaddeus wasn't himself."

"That's the truth," the old man piped in. "Haven't been myself for a long time now."

"I mean she'd be the only one who'd know that the man they'd substituted was an imposter. Everyone else could be fooled. Bankers, lawyers, the zoo commission, the people who run the preserve for timber wolves—all of them could be convinced it was really you, that you'd just changed your mind. But Miss Partridge would have to be gotten out of the way for the scheme to work."

Thaddeus shook his head and mused, "So that's why that snooty doctor wanted those pictures of me. All the while, I thought he was going to put me into Ripley's or something, for turning into a werewolf."

I'd had another thought. "Miss Partridge, did you ever mention to Miss Thaddeus that you hated the rats?"

The red veins in her eyes seemed to clear up a bit as she thought, hard. "Damned tootin' I did," she said. "Last time Jill was out here, we talked about them. She caught one of them nibbling at her shoestring and said something was going to have to be done about them. I agreed. She's the one suggested the rat poisoning, even told me where to get it!''

"Well, that doesn't look too good for her," I said, "but still, it doesn't mean she poisoned the wine herself or knew about it. But I'd bet you anything that the poison will turn out to be the same kind you bought to kill the rats with—and from the same store.''

Miss Partridge's eyes were bugging out now. "Damned tootin'," she said. "Jill told me her boyfriend said it was a good idea to get rid of the rats, said he told her they were bound to start another bubonic plague.''

"See?" said Thaddeus. "See what I mean? It's that sort of poppycock that got me to take the little critters in to begin with.''

"Hush up, you old coot. I'm going to get rid of those damned rats.''

I said, "Did Miss Thaddeus say anything else? Anything that might help?''

Miss Partridge thought, then said, "She told me the wine was a gift of appreciation for taking such good care of this old coot here. Seemed odd to me at the time, but wine is wine, and I'm not likely to turn any down.''

I didn't know if I believed her or not. It sounded a little like embroidery to me. Still, it fit the facts. I said, "Is there any way anyone else could have gotten in here? Do you keep the house locked?''

"Jill's got keys to all the doors. Tank did, too. No telling who they gave them to.''

"All right," I concluded, "both of you, be careful what you eat and drink for a while. I'd suggest you get rid of all foodstuffs and start from scratch.''

"Happy to," said Miss Partridge. "Everything here's got rat droppings in it anyway.''

"Mr. Thaddeus," I said, "would you like me to take your cat out and bury her in the back?''

"No need to, boy," replied Thaddeus. "We'll likely

have a little private service for her. After all, she was one of the family.''

A tear trickled from his eye, down his cheek, and into his thick gray beard.

CHAPTER
TWENTY-NINE

STOPPED AT A DELICATESSEN, PICKED UP A PASTRAMI and swiss on rye for lunch, then drove to my office.

As I unlocked my door, I noticed that the name I'd had painted on the pebbled glass was getting a little flaky. I sat down at my desk, opened the waxed paper, took out the sandwich, and started eating. It was greasy. I laid it to one side and turned on my answering machine.

Someone had called over and over again, without leaving a message. Then a growling voice came on. Taft. "Weatherby, you're one smart asshole, aren't you? Back down in Desolado playing cops and robbers, huh? We're looking for you." That was all, but it was enough.

The next message was from Angelo. He had something hot for me. Call him back ASAP.

I called Gerry at the clinic and asked about the Evans boy. She told me he was doing fine, had decided he wanted to stay for a while. He was in the swimming pool right then, but she'd tell him I'd called. I thanked her and promised I'd have some money for her tomorrow morning.

Next, I opened my telephone book, thumbed through the pages, and found the phone number of Marnie Evans.

She answered on the fourth ring. Her voice was lazy with sleep and artificially sexy. "Helloooo . . ."

"Afternoon, Mrs. Evans."

"Who is this?"

"This is Artie Weatherby and I need to see you."

"I'm very busy today."

"After all we've meant to each other? I have to talk to you about Brian."

"Brian who?"

"Brian, your stepson. Look, don't play games with me, Marnie. I know that you took my keys and made impressions of them. I know you were in my office. And I know a lot of other things, too."

Her voice was sharp, anxious. "Like what?"

"Like you're spending Brian's money on nose jobs and Venetian glass. He's in a jam. He needs help."

"Is this blackmail?"

"I prefer the word extortion. It sounds more professional."

"Sweetie, what in hell is this?" The first traces of real panic were in her voice now.

"Look, Marnie, your baked roses made me sick, you ripped off my keys so that your sleazebag boyfriend could pilfer my office and who knows what else, and I've figured out enough to know that there's bound to be some money in this for little old you-know-who, and I don't mean you."

"Sweetie"—her voice was oiled honey again—"I'm sorry I got mad because you puked. I should have been more understanding. You'll forgive little old Marnie, won't you? Pretty please?"

"Save it for Sterling, Marnie. I want cash. Cash and facts."

Her voice was flat again, flinty. "Or what?"

"Or I'll send photostatic copies of your plastic surgery files to every woman who belongs to your country club."

"What a nasty thing to say."

"I could send copies to all the scandal sheets in Europe, too. That should give the barons and baronesses something to chat about."

"You couldn't get my files. Sterling wouldn't let you have them."

"Too late." I flipped open the folder and began to read. I'd just gotten to the bottom of the first paragraph when she said, "Shut up! Just shut up! You louse, how could you do this to me?"

I said, "Easy as peacock pie. Throw on something comfortable. I'll be over in about twenty minutes."

I checked my .38 Special to make sure it was fully loaded, stuck it in my shoulder holster, put on my sweater, then dialed Angelo. "Hey, old buddy. I got your message."

"Weatherby! Where the hell've you been? You've been missing all the action. Guess what."

"What?"

"They're trying to get an indictment against Sterling for trafficking in cocaine."

"Yeah?"

"Yeah. Friend of mine at the courthouse told me."

"Who wants the papers, city cops or feds?"

"Whaddaya think? Feds, of course. Word is that Sterling's supposed to be the upper-crust's link to the coke being brought in by the Satan's Sadists. Feds want to bust him for possession and conspiracy to distribute."

"But they don't have the indictment yet?"

"Nah. Here's the dirt on that. Seems like the prosecutor handling the case belongs to the same country club as Sterling, doesn't think there's enough hard evidence to convict, doesn't want to go to trial. He's giving the boys in the field a hard time. Word is that they're going to get that indictment, though, no matter who they have to fry."

"Sterling's probably paying off some politician who's got the handle on the prosecutor's job," I said. "Happens all the time. Look, who exactly is trying to make the case?"

"Who else but your true-blue friends, amigo?"

"Taft and Tafoya?"

"The same. You knew they were investigating the Satan's Sadists."

"I couldn't figure out if they were investigating them or protecting them from being investigated. Hell, I'm still not sure. Anyway, thanks for the info, Angelo. Keep your eyes and ears open.''

CHAPTER
THIRTY

MARNIE TUCKED A GOLD-TIPPED CIGARETTE INTO A long carved ivory holder, put it between her moist violet lips, and leaned forward for a light. A canyon of cleavage showed at the top of her ice-pink scoop-necked lounging pajamas.

I shook my head. "Sorry, baby. I'm fresh out of matches."

She sat up in a huff, took a gold table lighter from atop the glass end table, flicked angrily at it until it burst into flame, then jammed the flame at the end of her cigarette. She puffed, took a drag, then blew smoke out in a tiny ribbon that curled upward like a vaporous lizard's tongue. When the smoke had drifted away, she said, "So now, Mr. Weatherby, what is this nonsense about my stepson?"

"The kid's strung out pretty bad. I took him to a clinic today. A couple of my friends run it. A good place. But it costs money to operate, so I figured you'd maybe pick up Brain's share of the tab, especially since you're just throwing his money away.

"*My* money, sweetie." She blew smoke at the ceiling. "My darling husband left it all to me. And it's none of your damned business how I spend it."

"I guess I'm just your average nosy do-gooder. But I have a strong feeling that the court would say otherwise."

"Oh, now you're threatening me with that?"

"Threat or fact. Take your choice. I'll take a check for ten thousand smackeroos. Make it out to Brian Evans. That'll take care of the tab at the clinic, plus give him a little cash for school and an apartment when he gets out. We'll take it from there after we get that far."

She stepped over to a white desk with gold leaf trim and said, "I'll give you your damned piddling check. And then I want the files."

I waited until she scribbled out the check and handed it to me, and then I said, "Okay so far. Now I need something else."

She was using her flat, flinty voice again. "What now?"

"I want to know why you ripped off my keys and broke into my office."

"I didn't."

"Come on, Marnie. I have a witness."

Blood drained from her already pale face. "No-nobody could know that—"

"But Sterling," I finished for her. "Come on, Marnie. He's setting you up to take the fall for him."

"That bastard!"

"Why don't you tell me your version of what happened? What's your connection to that guy?"

"He's—he *was*—my doctor."

"And your lover?"

"No."

"He says otherwise." It was an old ploy, but it seemed to be working.

"That *bastard*! Yes, I was dumb enough to let him make love to me." Her false eyelashes were heavy and thick, like the fat black legs of a tarantula. She laid them down low over her high cheekbones, swooped them up and down a couple of times, and said, "Oh, sweetie, you have to help me! I didn't mean to get mixed up in all of this. It just happened. Sterling—he's—he's—"

"Spit it out, kid."

With a defiant gesture, she pulled up the sleeve of her pajamas, opened her arm, and showed me the soft pink-white flesh of her forearm. The inside of her elbow was covered with track marks, some of them old scars, others brand-new dewdrops of scab. I felt my jaw tighten as I said, "He has you strung out."

She nodded. "I'm not the only one. A lot of the girls at the country club . . ." She let the thought trail off.

"Why?"

"He knows, sweetie. He *knows* what it's like to grow old in a town where youth and beauty are the only things that matter. He knows, too, that the face lifts and chemical peels aren't enough. He—he—" She started sobbing.

I waited for her to pull herself back together, then I said, "Why don't you just tell me all of it, and we'll see what we can do."

She smoothed a stray strand of platinum hair and said, "Will you pour me a snifter of brandy?" She pointed toward a crystal decanter with matching glasses on top of a highboy. I poured her brandy. When I'd handed her the snifter and she'd taken a gulp that drained the glass, she seemed a little steadier. She said, "I guess I might as well tell you. We had an affair. While I was still married, back when he did my nose. Sterling blackmailed me. He took pictures—oh, he's such a bastard—and told me that he'd show them to my husband if I didn't give him money. He was in quite a jam at the time, sweetie. He had several people suing him. I was stupid. I sold some real estate my husband had—I actually forged his name—and gave the money to Worth. And then I got away from him."

"And?"

"And then I decided to have my chin lifted, and Worth *is* the best doctor in town."

"Then why is he always being sued?"

She brushed at that strand of hair again. "Oh, sometimes he just doesn't care. When he's just after the money, he does as many as ten operations in a day. He gets tired—tired of whiny old bags is what he told me. But when he wants to be, he's a miracle man. So I went back to him, and before I realized it, we were having another affair. Then my husband was killed, and Worth was right there when I needed him—''

"How much did he soak you for *that*?''

"I sold some stocks and bonds. He said he owed money to his lawyers. It wasn't until later that I found out he was buying cocaine. Some of the girls at the club started talking to me about it. They were buying from him.''

"They talked about it there?''

"Several of them had had affairs with Worth. Yes, they talked about everything he did. I knew he had laid a lot of them and gotten serious with a few. I even knew he was supposedly engaged to that Thaddeus girl, Jill. But I could never take that very seriously. I mean, she's such a vapid, sexless little thing. She has the personality of a hard-boiled egg. Fill my snifter, would you, sweetie? Thank you. I— for some reason I couldn't seem to give Sterling up. Of course, I was heavy into the coke by then. And—well, here I am.'' She stared sadly into her snifter. "Little old Marnie in the middle of some big bad trouble that I don't understand. I believed him, you know. He said that—that—''

"Spit it out, kid.''

"He said that he wanted to marry me. That the reason he hadn't paid any of the money back was that he'd put a down payment on a little old castle on the Rhine, where we'd live after we got married. I believed him. Until—''

"Until what?''

"Until I caught him humping my best friend, Lucinda, in the shower room at the club. When I confronted her later, she told me that he'd been saying and doing the same things to her that he had to me. And then I knew he was lying, of course, about everything. But it's hard to be all alone in this big bad world, sweetie. And of course I wanted the cocaine. Suddenly he seemed to get very serious about me. He told me he realized that being with Jill was a mistake. He'd tried to break it off entirely so that we could get married, but she started giving him a hard time. I knew, of course, that he was involved in the cocaine thing by then. He told me that Jill suspected that he was getting his coke from her brother and those other bikers out in the desert. He said he'd picked up the phone one day and over-heard her talking to some lousy shamus—that must have been you, sweetie—who she'd hired to snoop on him. He was worried about what she'd do when she found out about the coke—she'd heard rumors at the club, of course. So he asked me to get an impression of your keys—he even showed me how to do it—and then we could sneak into your office and find out what you were really up to. I didn't realize how rotten things really were until we stepped into your office and saw that awful *thing* sitting in your chair."

"You mean Tank Thaddeus?"

She had a strange look on her face as she nodded. She swallowed hard and said, "I thought I'd seen some sicko stuff, but I've never seen anything like that before. I still have nightmares about it. We turned around and got right back out of there."

"Did Sterling know who he was? The corpse, I mean."

She nodded and smoothed the satin pajamas against her leg. "He told me it was Jill's brother."

"Did Sterling seem afraid? Worried?"

She shook her head. "No. He seemed—well, if any-thing, he seemed mad as hell."

"Did he say anything?"

She thought long and hard, then a tiny hint of anticipated revenge curled into the corners of her mouth. "He said something that I didn't pay much attention to at the time. But it might mean something to you. He said, 'Why in bloody hell does that bloodsucking McNulty have to screw up everything he does? Every move he makes, he leaves tracks.' Does that help you, sweetie?"

I gave her my poker face and said, "Some. I'd like to know, Marnie. Did you keep the keys you had made, or does Sterling have them?"

"Worth took the impressions. I never saw the actual keys until that night we went to your office."

"And he just used them at the front door? My office was already open?"

"Yes. Your office door was slightly open."

Things were starting to fall into place now.

Nails had killed Tank Thaddeus, almost certainly at Sterling's demand. Tank had finally decided to blow the whistle on Sterling's scheme to clone old man Thaddeus and have the clone sign over everything to Jill. Nails had either brought him there (if Sterling had given Nails the keys) or followed him there (if the keys had been given to Tank Thaddeus). Either way, Tank ended up dead. Sometimes when the bikers made a hit on a squealer, they cut his penis out and stuck it in his mouth. Sometimes they slit his throat. Tank had been ready to talk, all right. And unless I missed my guess, the reason the hit had been made in my office was that they wanted to scare me off the case. Some people will do a lot for the white nose candy. Others will do a lot more for twenty million dollars. . . .

I said, "Thanks, kid. You've been a big help." I stood up.

She jumped to her feet, too. "What about my files?"

"Maybe I'd better just hang on to them long enough to make sure the check doesn't bounce."

"I don't see why you're meddling in my relationship with Brian. The brat hates me. How on earth did you find out about him?"

"Serendipity." I took a step toward the door.

"I want my files. You promised me."

"You'll get them. Later." I paused with my hand on the doorknob.

"You bastard. You're as bad as Worth. I should have known when you puked that night that you'd never know how to treat a woman decently. I should have used my gun on you today. I thought about it. I should have put a bullet straight through your pecker when I had the chance."

Gently, I closed the door behind me.

CHAPTER
THIRTY-ONE

STRAUSSLER'S CLINIC WAS A SPRAWLING SPANKING-NEW building on east Woodlawn Drive, about a half hour's drive from Marnie's. The nurse at the reception desk escorted me into Gerry's office. Gerry paged Brian, who met us there.

He'd already been through detox. They'd cut his hair. He was looking a whole lot better. "He's been eating," Gerry bubbled. She stood up, came around the desk, and tousled his hair. He looked pleased and embarrassed all at the same time. She said, "Look! He's already put on a pound or two. Turning into a good-looking kid, isn't he?"

The expression on his face made me laugh. To him, I said, "Not so bad here, huh?"

He grinned and shrugged his shoulders. Gerry's motherly, freckled face took on its professional look and she said, "Now it's just a matter of therapy. We have a big job ahead of us. Brian must realize that most of what happened wasn't his fault. But the parts that were his fault—well, we have to make him understand and accept that, too. We'd like to keep him here at least a month, Artie. Is there a problem with that? With his stepmother?"

I shook my head. "No. In fact, here's a check from her. And a little extra to help take care of him when he gets out. We can get him an apartment, get him in school—or he can stay with me, for that matter. Although I'm not home much.''

"We've talked about that already," she said. "He's welcome to stay with us, too. We have so much extra room in that big old house now that our own kids are in college.''

Brian's face was overcast. He said, "I bet she didn't want to give you anything—the money, I mean.''

"Marnie doesn't know what she wants, Brian. She's twice as messed up as you'll ever be.''

Gerry shook her head sadly. "It seems that that's most often the case. Parents are so often incapable of parenting.''

Brian's eyes flashed anger. "She's not my parent! My dad was only married to her for a year before he got killed. Don't call her my mother! Not even my stepmother!''

I said, "Okay, kid. You don't have to live with her, or even see her if you don't want to. Gerry and I both know good lawyers. We'll get your father's money for you, and we'll get her out of your hair. We'll work it out.''

I told them that if the check bounced, or if they had any other problems, to call me right away, then I drove to my office.

The day was sultry. Dry. The building looked shabby in the harsh afternoon sunlight. Inside, the corridor looked shabbier. The paint on the window of my office door was still flaky, and inside the lingering smell of ammonia stung my nostrils. I crossed the office and opened the windows.

Then I turned on my answering machine. Only one message. Call Jill Thaddeus, urgent. I dialed her number. For a change, she answered right away. Sterling wasn't there. She needed to talk to me desperately, but she refused to give any details on the phone. She'd learned that Sterling had been eavesdropping on her phone calls and even though he was gone, she was paranoid. Could we meet somewhere? I gave her my home address and told her to be there at five. She agreed.

Next, I filtered through the junk mail, tossed it in the

trash can, then put my feet up on my desk and stared at the ceiling.

The spider was still there.

The web was twice as big today, and the spider looked twice as big, too. Maybe I didn't like that spider after all. I climbed up on my desk, knocked it to the floor, smashed it with a flyer I retrieved from the wastebasket, then I sat back down at my desk.

I looked at my watch. Only one o'clock. Jill had to drive clear across town, stop at her father's, then drive back and up the canyon to my place. It would be four hours before I'd see her. It had been just twelve sweet hours since I'd heisted the files from Dr. Worthington Sterling's office. Three hours since Thaddeus's cat had been killed.

I put my feet back up on the desk and thought about that for a while. Some of the pieces of the puzzle were finally falling together. But some still didn't fit. Or did they?

It was certain now that Sterling was linked to the Satan's Sadists. The reasons for that were no mystery.

Two types of people make up the majority of the coke-heads and other hard-drug users: social dropouts, like Bunny and Tank and the rest of the bikers; and the *nouveau riche*, with too much money and time on their hands and no sense of social responsibility. Sterling's crowd. The doc had cut himself a sweet deal, if your sweetener was money and plastic sex with plastic people. He had his little remodeling tools and his white stuff, and enough phony charm to make him a movie star if he wanted it. But he'd evidently stumbled across an even sweeter deal with Jill Thaddeus and her dotty old father.

And he'd cooked up a scheme, all right. The question was, what part did Jill play in it?

And what about Marnie Evans? I was sure she'd told me the truth. She wasn't *that* stupid. She was trying to get out. She'd probably figured out that she amounted to a little interim financing while the good Doctor Feelgood was putting the big act together. Twenty million dollars.

If my little gray cells were right, Jill Thaddeus was safe for the moment. And she'd be safe until Sterling had finished his remodeling job on Robert Graves, the new clone—until Graves had forged all the necessary papers. At which time, Jill Thaddeus was going to be sleeping the big siesta.

I locked up my office, then ran some long-avoided errands. I got my laundry from the cleaners, gassed up my car, stopped by the bank and ordered some checks. Still time to kill. I got a haircut. Then I stopped by the supermarket, then I drove home.

Three-thirty.

I took a shower, shaved, then cooked myself a steak sandwich and made a salad. When I was through, my watch said a quarter till five.

I was restless. I called the Thaddeus mansion. Miss Partridge answered. The old man was out back with his timber wolves. Jill had stopped by for a few moments, then left. She hung up on me when I started to ask her if she'd contacted the doctor I'd recommended.

I phoned Angelo to see if he had an update. He'd already left the office for the day, and he hadn't yet arrived home. I switched on the TV, switched it back off again. I checked my watch. Five-fifteen.

I called Sterling's clinic. His office nurse said he was in surgery and wouldn't be free until around eight. I didn't leave a message.

It was a quarter till six and the setting sun was just edging gold into the scrub oak along the canyon walls when I heard a car zooming up the road. I went to the front window and pulled the drapes. Jill Thaddeus turned into my driveway and her car purred to a stop. She climbed from behind the wheel and walked up the short, flagstone walkway, patting her hair nervously.

She looked sleek, polished, expensive. Her auburn hair was pulled severely back from her face. As she got close to the door and reached out to touch the bell, I could see worry in her eyes. I opened the door as she hit the bell for the second time.

"Sorry I'm late. The traffic—"

"I admit I was getting worried. Make yourself comfortable."

She sat down in an easy chair, put her purse on the end table, and crossed her legs. "I'm very glad you called," she said. "I've been at my wit's end."

"I've about reached mine, too," I said. "You haven't helped much. Look, would you like something to drink?"

"No, thank you."

"Then let's get down to business. Why did you really hire me, Miss Thaddeus?"

"I—I suppose I was afraid."

"Of what?"

"I don't know. Something was wrong, and I didn't know what. Sometimes I'd catch Sterling looking at me so strangely, and then he got this bizarre idea about having somebody pretend to be Father and sign everything over to us so that Father couldn't disinherit me. And he seemed to be such good friends with those bikers. He started going out to the desert all the time, and he wouldn't let me go with him, but I figured he was seeing Tank. And then some of the girls at the club started talking about him having something to do with cocaine—"

"He's a major trafficker, Miss Thaddeus. You might as well know that up front. He's been scamming you so he can get to your money."

"Yes. Well, I—" A little sob caught in her throat. "I suppose I shouldn't be surprised at hearing you say it. I've suspected as much for a long time."

"He was sleeping with other women, Miss Thaddeus. And lying to them, and using them, too."

"I'd heard as much. Several of the girls at the club—"

"After marrying you, he'd almost certainly have killed you. He's responsible for Tank's death."

"I—I'd wondered."

"And you stayed with him?"

"I've been afraid of what he'd do if he knew how much I suspected. That's why I let him fire you."

"So now we have the bad news out of the way. Here's some good news. Your father isn't turning into a were-wolf."

Her eyes opened up wide. "I already knew that."

"He's not crazy, either."

"But—then—"

"What's wrong with him? He's ill, Miss Thaddeus. He has a very rare disease known as porphyria. I'm almost positive. He has all the symptoms. It's just a matter of getting him to a doctor for treatment."

"It can be treated?" She looked disbelieving and dazed.

"I'll give you the number of a physician who is an authority on the disease. You and your father can take it from there."

She suddenly put her hands over her face and burst into tears. I let her cry it out, then I said, "We won't be able to bring Tank back, but other than that, things are going to be all right, Miss Thaddeus."

She was snuffling. "Mr. Weatherby, help me get rid of Sterling, help me get him out of my life. Please, please. I'm afraid of him."

"I'll help you. But I need to know something else. Someone put cyanide in the wine you took Miss Partridge. I suppose they told you?"

"It was the truth? They mentioned it, yes, and they told me they'd already had the service for Father's tabby. They were angry because I hadn't come, though they didn't bother to call me, but—but they're always jabbering about the strangest things, and when Miss Partridge accused me of trying to poison her, I thought it was just more of her nonsense."

"There *was* cyanide in the wine, Miss Thaddeus."

She said bitterly, "Sterling gave me that wine. He told me to take it to Miss Partridge, that we needed her on our side. He seems able to get me to do anything these days. I swear I didn't know the wine was poisoned though.

"I believe you," I said. "Listen, I have to drive back to the desert and check out a few things. Why don't you stay here for the night? That way you'll be away from Sterling. It might be harder for you to pretend not to know anything now. But I want to nail him to the wall, Miss Thaddeus. I ripped off some files from his office last night—"

"So that's why he was so angry today!"

"When I get back from the desert, I want you to call him and deliver a message. Will you do that for me?"

"I'm afraid of him."

"All you have to do is speak to him on the phone."

"He's really a frightening man, isn't he? I mean, he's so very different from the way he pretended to be at first. Yes, Mr. Weatherby. Yes, I'll help you."

CHAPTER
THIRTY-TWO

IT WAS ONE OF THOSE COLD, CLEAR DESERT NIGHTS. THE dark, bleak highway stretched out before me. Once in a long while a pair of headlights would appear on the horizon. When the driver was close enough, he'd hit the dimmer and the headlights would beam down. And then the car or truck would grind toward and past me and I'd be alone again.

A sliver of moon outlined the low bluffs and the haunted outcroppings of rock. The light etched out the ghostly forms of the saguaros and the sagebrush, of the eerie, grotesquely human outlines of the Joshua trees.

I had time to think during the drive from the city. By the time I saw the first, faint mist of light that told me I was approaching Desolado, I had a lot of things figured out.

It was only nine-thirty. I drove past Sandy's gaudy pink neon, past old man Tucker's night-enshrouded store. I drove through the five blocks of storefronts, one-story houses, and streetlights that formed the town, and then I was on the south side, driving past the little cafe where I had first seen my golden lady love. Damn. Dreams die hard. I was having a tough time accepting her as cold and

ruthless enough to be a cocaine trafficker. Where, oh, where
are the girls of yesteryear?

When I was a quarter of a mile from the Cactus Corners
Motel and Garage, I doused my car lights. I drove slowly
then—the moon didn't give much light. I'd noticed some
rutted tracks at the side of the highway when I'd made my
great escape the last time I'd been here. I watched for
them, found them, Sure enough, it was a sort of road. I
followed it, my car bouncing through the ruts and over the
bumps, but in no time at all I was hidden from the buildings by a small upthrust of sandstone.

I checked my gun and my flashlight. After locking the
car, I moved slowly, carefully, toward the buildings.

There was a dim light in the empty lobby, and other
lights in the adjoining unit. I didn't bother to check in.

The two hot-pink mopeds sat in front of the end unit
where Tank and Bunny had lived in connubial bliss. The
windows were dark. In fact, only two of the units seemed
occupied, both with lights in the windows. One had a new
Chevette parked in front of it. The other was occupied by
someone who was driving a black '83 Jeep Cherokee. Both
vehicles had Arizona plates. As I moved closer, I could
hear the sounds of gunfire coming from a television set
inside the first unit.

I knew the lay of the land better than I had the first time.
I crept past the pink stucco building and looped around and
between the motel and the ramshackle house. I was careful
to stay in the shadows, to melt into their outlines as I
moved. I'd learned how when I'd been with Special Forces
in Nam. I was damned good at that sort of thing. Someone
staring straight at me would have missed me.

The windows in the garage were black, but that same,
bare death-house lightbulb illuminated the sign.

I crept past the garage and over to the house. It was
ablaze with light and the sounds of voices and laughter
wafted out of a half-open window. There was a battered
red pickup truck parked in front of the house. Beside it
were four choppers, all of them black with lots of chrome

and with Satan's Sadists emblems painted on their bodies. I stood on tiptoe and looked in the window.

Nails and Crystal were there, laying out lines of coke onto a large square of black construction paper. Crystal picked up some of the white powder, using the long nail of her little finger, and touched it to her tongue. She made a face. "They used too much ether when they purified it," she said.

Nails dug one grease-rimmed fingernail into his straggling brown hair, scratched. "Does that mean it's no good?"

"It's good, all right. Just not quite as pure as they want us to think."

"How pure is it?"

"Seventy to eighty percent. Pure enough so that everybody along the line can step on it a few times and it'll still have *some* coke in it when it hits the streets. Are you gonna cut this stuff with meth like you did the last batch?"

"If it's pure enough."

"It is."

"Let's blow a line or two."

"Not me. I need to keep my head clear so I can check the other kilos. These two bastards tried to short us on the last shipment, remember?"

Nails nodded.

He pulled a long chain out from under his soiled T-shirt. It held a tiny coke spoon. He dipped it into the coke, held one nostril closed with one finger and snorted the coke, then dipped the spoon in again and sniffed it up the other nostril. He did that several times, then he dropped the spoon back beneath his T-shirt and started twisting at his nose, unscrewing it from his face, in the universal language of the cokehead. His face had paled a shade or two and his eyes, although wider, were more bleary. When he talked, it came out in a rapid staccato. "Yes, you're right, Crystal. That's some pretty good shit. Let's make the buy."

"That's my advice," she agreed.

Just then, Bunny came into the room. Her huge breasts were squeezing up and out of a hot-pink tanktop. "C'mon,

Nails," she whined. "How much longer is this crap gonna take? I wanna go to Sandy's an' shoot some pool with Barney, that cute trucker."

"Shaddup, Bunny," barked Nails.

She put her hands on her hips, tilted her head, and said, "Screw you, Nails. You actin' like a big shot ever since you did the number on Tank. If he was still alive—"

He glared at her. "You miss Tank so much, I'll fix it so's you're with him."

Crystal looked disgusted. "Man, will you two ever stop fighting? Get serious, Bunny. You know that nobody comes or goes here until after the buy goes down and they've picked the cars up. Why don't you do a line, mellow yourself out?"

"Screw you, Crystal. You probably want Barney for yourself! Just because Nails listens to your damned dumb ideas doesn't mean you're *my* boss." She shot Crystal a lethal look and swung back through the door.

Nails said, "Someday Bunny's gonna bring heat down on us."

Crystal was scooping coke back into a plastic bag. "She's pretty loose about things, all right."

Nails was edgy, coked out. "If anyone ever brings heat down on me, I'll cut their nuts off and feed 'em to 'em."

"Bunny doesn't have nuts anymore."

Nails flexed his muscles. "I'll chop off her tits, then. I hate those narcs. Hate 'em. Especially them feds. It's because of some stupid snitch that I done time. He balled up his fist; the tendons on his neck stuck out as he growled, "I'd kill any fed that come close to me—kill 'em, kill 'em!" His eyes were wild.

Crystal gave him a bored look. "Nails, I told you, I've got them paid off. Relax, will you? I'm going to run some more tests on this stuff, just to verify the purity. Then you can go tell Pedro it's a buy. C'mon, Nails, you've got a tidy profit of half a million bucks about to fall into your pocket, and you're wailing away about the feds?"

He brightened some. "I'll be able to send Ma on that trip to Paris she's always wanted." He looked beatific.

Crystal was setting up some vials full of colored chemicals on the table. Matter-of-factly, she said, "That's right. You do have some nice plans for her, don't you?"

"Ma's always waited for this day. She started way back when, bringing in the grass from the Mexes. But she never made the big time. It's nice to have her so proud of me."

I took one last look at my ladylove, then I hunched down below the window and crept on past the house.

The sawhorse was right where I'd left it, behind the motel. I picked it up, carried it over to beneath the lighted window of the first motel unit, then carefully set it down.

When I climbed up, I was staring through the window and down at a large Hispanic man. He was stretched out on the bed. His eyes were closed. The television was on, its electronic patter barely audible through the window glass.

His brown loafers were beside the bed. He had on gray socks with an unusual pattern: little black and white pocket watches. He had his slacks on, though they were unzipped partway. His white dress shirt was unbuttoned at the collar and wrinkled, as if he'd slept in it more than this once. A holstered gun hung on the back of a chair, atop a gray jacket. He had salt-and-pepper hair and a swarthy, pockmarked face that needed a shave. I could see his chest rise and fall as he breathed deeply, then exhaled, then breathed deeply again. Every once in a while his breath seemed to catch in his throat and his chest heaved, then he'd snore.

I stepped down from the sawhorse, lifted it carefully, and moved on down the row. The next window looked into the kitchenette of the same unit.

A young Latino sat beside the kitchen table. He was watching the TV I'd heard from the other room. He wore a khaki shirt and pants, and there were about twelve kilos of white stuff sealed into cellophane packages and stacked on the table beside him. An Uzi submachine gun was lying across his legs, which were propped up on another kitchen chair. He was smoking a brown cigarette. Laughter came from the TV, and he laughed, too. I looked at the screen. *Leave It to Beaver*. Wally was telling the Beaver how to

cope with life. The Beaver frowned and said something to
Wally that I couldn't quite make out.

I watched the man carefully for a full five minutes. He
didn't do anything, just sat there guarding the dope. Once
he took a toothpick out of his shirt pocket and went to work
on his yellowed teeth.

Carefully, silently, I stepped down off the sawhorse.
Okay, Weatherby. So you've bumped into a major dope
buy. So what? Now what was I going to do?

I picked up the sawhorse, and carried it back to where
I'd found it. I moved back toward the house, darting from
shadow to shadow as I moved. I got to the side of the house
and melted into the shadows, then started to turn the corner.

"Ooof!" The sound came from whatever or whoever I'd
crashed into. I reached out to catch my balance, and I
latched on to something that was hard and soft at the same
time. I jerked back, my hand automatically going for my
.38 Special, and then I was blinking my eyes once, twice.

Crystal stood there, eye to eye and nose to nose with
me.

Her whisper was a hiss. "Oh, no, of all the rotten things
to happen."

I whispered back, "You don't seem very glad to see
me."

"Be quiet!" She gritted her teeth and twisted the words
out. "You are the worst damned thing that has ever happened to me. Why in hell can't you stay away?" And then
I felt something hard shove into my ribs, something as hard
and round as the barrel of a gun, and the look in her eyes
was telling me that she was having a hard time keeping
herself from pulling the trigger.

It was enough to make my macho go soft.

She prodded me with the gun. "This way, brother. And
move! You may think you're tough, but you sure as hell
aren't bulletproof." She prodded me harder. "I said
move!"

I felt an electric tension from her body. This girl was
wired tight. She just might pull that trigger. I moved.

She kept her gun on me as we went around the back of the house and toward the farthest edge of the stripped-out cars. She hesitated, then stopped for just an instant as if trying to decide something, then she said out loud, "Look, shamus, you apparently don't have any idea what you've fallen into. I'm going to give you one more chance. If I let you go, will you promise to go straight to wherever you parked your car and quietly get the hell out of here?"

I said, "I love you."

She said, "Oh, sure. You're going to get me killed, you prick. I'm going to tell you one more time: Get out of Desolado and stay out. Because if I catch you slithering around out here anymore, I'm going to turn you over to Nails and the Seven Perverts and tell him that I have proof that you're working for the feds."

"Woman, that would be a low thing to do."

"Keep your voice down. Can't you see that you're going to get yourself killed and me with you? Get out of here. Now." She stamped a dainty foot and pulled back the hammer on her gun.

I thought about taking the gun away from her. Tell you the truth, I'd *been* thinking about it ever since she'd pulled it on me. But the girl was good. She stayed just far enough away from me, just at the right angle. I hate to admit it, but I couldn't figure out a way to do anything but draw my little .38 and shoot it out with her, and that seemed a little extreme, since all she wanted me to do was vamoose.

Oh, well. It wasn't the first time I'd been shined off by a pretty face. It wouldn't be the last. "My car is parked behind those rocks over there. I guess I'll just go quietly over there and get in it."

"Damn," she said. She turned her head to watch the headlights of what appeared to be two trucks coming down the highway. "I have to go. You just get to your car and wait there till the trucks have loaded up and gone. You'll be safe."

"You really care," I said.

"Move your ass, fool. We're running out of time."

She slipped back around the house. I moved stealthily

past the garage, then, when I was on the far side, I stopped and waited. I heard the sound of gears grinding down. The two semis pulled into the gravel lot in front of the garage. Two men got out, leaving the engines running, and several of the bikers, including Nails, came out of the house to greet them. I could hear their voices above the noise from the engines, but I couldn't make out the words.

The lights went on in the garage. There was a metallic gnashing as someone slid the wide double doors open. I could see several cars inside.

Crystal came back into view. She was walking toward the garage, coming from the direction of the motel. Both of the Latinos were with her. They were all talking. I could see that the younger one was still carrying the machine gun, while Crystal and the older one were carrying the kilos of cocaine. The older man reached out and patted her on the backside. She jerked away and seemed to say something sharp.

I ducked deeper into the shadows and kicked back to watch the show.

CHAPTER
THIRTY-THREE

ONE OF THE TRUCK DRIVERS SWUNG UP AND INTO THE tractor of his rig. With a growl of the engine and a grinding of gears, he had her in motion, backing around in a jack-knife so that the trailer was coming up in front of the garage door. Headlights swept the desert night as it moved, then swept across the place where I'd been standing the second before I'd dropped to my belly.

The truck stopped with a hiss of air brakes, and the driver opened the door. He dropped to the ground without disturbing the cigarette dangling from his lips. Two bikers who'd been guiding him stepped forward and laid a metal ramp from the ground in front of the garage door and up into the trailer.

There was the tiny metal purr of an expensive engine starting, and then a new Rolls-Royce came out the garage door, Nails behind the wheel. The silver paint on it was so new it shimmered. I watched as a hundred thousand dollars' worth of wheels went up the ramp and into the dark belly of the trailer. Nails reappeared in the door of the trailer, jumped to the ground, and went back into the garage.

Crystal and the two Hispanics were still together, standing off to one side but still in the light. Jonesie, Snake, and

Lester the Molester had joined them. Envelopes were changing hands—probably money and the phony papers for the cars.

Nails tooled a shiny red Mercedes out of the garage, stopped it on a dime, backed it up neatly—showing off for the boys—then wheeled it onto the ramp and up into the trailer.

My breath stopped as I froze. Something had crunched lightly, faintly, in the gravel behind me.

My eyes were the only things about me that were still moving, including my heart. My eyeballs shifted from side to side, trying to see what was going on behind me.

Damn! I couldn't see a thing. I held steady for a long moment, then turned around slowly. My heart lurched once, then seemed to stop again as I saw them.

Two shadowed figures were creeping stealthily from the back of the garage. They were crouched low, professionally trained. Both of them carried machine guns. With every step they took they stopped, poised and ready to fire.

Adrenaline flooded my body, turning the sudden lump in my throat into a tensed readiness. My hand found the reassuring cold metal of my gun.

But they weren't coming at me.

They stood straight up, melting into the garage wall, inching closer and closer to the open, lighted area where the bikers counted kilos of coke.

The figures looked familiar. What the—? No two forms looked alike. No two people moved alike. I *did* know them. It was Taft and Tafoya.

Well, well, well. My two friendly neighborhood feds, out for a friendly ripoff. I relaxed and almost laughed out loud. Crystal might have paid them off, but evidently she hadn't paid enough.

No wonder they'd been so eager to get me out of the picture! These two boys were lean and mean, and they weren't planning to retire on what they could make working for the federal government.

Carefully, I moved backward, watching them closely to make sure they hadn't seen the motion. They were intent

on the scenario in front of the garage. I angled my way
around two piles of rusting parts, then I slithered between
the junked-out bodies of automobiles, into the graveyard.
I leaned into the outline of a wrecked Mark IV and stopped.

I was still close enough to see them—all of them—and
close enough to use my gun if I needed to. But I was well
hidden. It was a nice feeling.

I watched Taft and Tafoya moving in like cats, poising
on the balls of their feet, stroking their machine guns as if
they were babies. I was actually anticipating the fireworks.

Crystal's angry shout spun me back around. Then she
screamed, a razor's edge of rage slicing through the words:
"Get your fucking hands off me!"

A scuffle had broken out between her and the two Latinos. Nails was climbing out of the car he'd just driven out
of the garage. My rented red Toyota—the bastards hadn't
even bothered to repaint it! One of the truckers was running
toward them, too. Crystal yelled again, "Get away from
me!"

"No, señorita," said one of her tormentors. "You some
sweet meat, 'ey? I theenk we take you back across the
border. You be our, how you say, een-surance, no?" His
laugh was like a rumble of thunder.

Nails had reached them. "What's going on?" he said
loudly.

Crystal was shouting, "No way, sleazebag! Get your
hands off my arm!"

My fist hardened around my gun. I forgot about Taft and
Tafoya, forgot about everything. I lunged toward Crystal—
and straight into a granite wall.

The wall moved. It was shoving me back, and then it
was crunching over me and pushing me to the ground.
Taft's voice was a rasping whisper right in my ear: "You
asshole. You trying to get her killed?"

Tafoya said, "Shut up, Taft. I can't hear!" He stuck a
little earplug back into his ear. He hit the radio on his belt
and turned on the sound to a police radio?

What the hell?

To Taft, I said, "Let me up. You're breaking my neck."

"You're damned right I am," he said.

"C'mon, Taft," said Tafoya." Cut the guy's nuts out later. Right now we got work to do."

Taft let go of me, saying, "Stay put, or I'll turn this machine gun on you and empty it."

Tafoya held up a finger. "One . . ."

The scuffle was still going on. The bikers, Nails included, were doing nothing to help her out. In fact, Nails was talking to the younger Hispanic and he was nodding his head, agreeing to something. I was sitting up far enough to be able to see but not so far that I'd annoy Taft. I rubbed at the place where he'd crunched the back of my head into the gravel.

Tafoya held up his finger again. "Two . . ."

I said, "Would someone mind telling me what the hell is going on?"

"Three!"

Six sets of car lights blazed to life behind us, and I turned my head in time to see six cars zooming out of the automobile graveyard, each with at least two men hanging out of the windows, each man aiming and firing a submachine gun, the rapid staccato of sound ripping through the air. The cars made a circle around the floodlit gravel in front of the garage, pinning in the trucks, the cars, the people.

Crystal had hit the ground. The Latinos ran this way then that, trying to find an escape. Stunned, the bikers sprinted around, some of them taking refuge in the garage, some pulling guns and knives and falling on their bellies in the gravel.

Taft and Tafoya had sprinted into the middle of the action on the count of three. I was left behind, sitting there on my can and watching the fireworks all right, but not exactly enjoying it.

The men were out of the cars now, shoving people up against the garage walls and cuffing them, chasing after fleeing bikers. I was standing, trying to figure it all out, when I saw Crystal.

She had rolled out of the middle of the floodlit parking

lot and halfway hidden herself under the trailer of one of the trucks. Her gun was in her hand and she had a wild yet somehow happy look on her face. Two bikers ran past her, yelled something at her, their own guns in their hands. She yelled something back and they went on by, then two machine-gun-wielding men—Taft's troops—ran after them. Crystal gave them a thumbs-up sign. Then the older Latino emerged from beneath the trailer, halfway crawling. He held a machine gun in one hand and tackled Crystal with the other, catching her from behind and throwing her to the ground.

He'd caught her off guard, and she still had her gun, but he moved forward, then chopped the machine gun down on her hand. Her gun went flying. Her face was white with terror and I could see that she was trying to scream, but the noises of shouting, gunshots, and engines revving were a waterfall of noise over it.

He grabbed one of her breasts, and his face gaped open in a horrible laugh. She struggled. He brought the machine gun up, started to bring it down on her skull, and I reacted. Feet paced wide, gun held steady in front of me, I fired.

He paused in mid-motion, almost as if something had just happened that puzzled him. At the same time, a small red hole appeared in the dead center of his forehead. A sudden fountain of blood gushed from the hole as he sagged, then fell to earth, taking Crystal with him.

In a second I was there, hoisting a thick, fat arm off her chest, pulling her up. She stared at me in astonishment, those emerald eyes still trapped in terror. Then there was awareness in them. She was alert again, though her voice held a stunned quality as she said, "Weatherby? I thought you were my father!"

"Father?"

She broke away from me easily and started moving dazedly toward the garage. "Dad? Dad?" Then a sort of panic took her voice as a new burst of gunfire came from inside the garage. She screamed, "Dad!" and started for the doorway, but a group of men ran out. They'd surrounded Jonesie, Snake, and Stinky, who were all handcuffed and chained together. Taft was in the lead, tromping along like a bull in heat.

I felt something move behind me, then someone had my hands and there was the feeling more than the sound of a soft click. Someone had put the cuffs on me. A gun was shoved into my back. I tried to turn around, but the gun dug in deep.

I was too confused to struggle. Then I heard Tafoya's voice, somewhere behind me. "Not that one, Ike. He's on our side." The cuffs were removed. I turned to see a thin, steely man in a flak jacket with big yellow lettering—Police—on the back. As he walked on past me, making for one of the bikers, he said, "Sorry, sir."

And then the feds and county police had them all collared. They were shoving them into the backseats of government cars. Taft stood a short distance from them, his arms around Crystal. She was talking to him, urgently. There was a familiarity, an intimacy, between them that sent a surge of jealousy through me.

I turned, started to walk away. Taft shouted, "Weatherby!"

Still walking, my back still to them, I said loudly, "What now?"

He cleared his throat, then said, "I just wanted to thank you for helping my little girl out of that jam."

I stopped. Little girl?

Slowly, I turned around to look at them. I guess he thought the expression on my face was funny, because his square, granite face cracked into a grin. He put his arm around Crystal's waist and they stepped up to me. He said, "Meet my daughter. DEA Special Agent Jane Taft—undercover name Crystal. Taffy is head of the U.S. Department of Justice's undercover operation, code-named Operation Snow White."

CHAPTER
THIRTY-FOUR

I LEFT THEM THERE, MOPPING UP, AND DROVE TO SANdy's Tavern. I used the pay phone to call Jill Thaddeus.

I told her to call Sterling and tell him to meet me at my office at midnight. To tell him that I had his files but that I'd give them back for a small fee. I figured he'd understand that.

She agreed to give Sterling my message. I waited at the bar and drank a 7-Up. Mabel evidently worked the day shift. The bartender tonight was her husband, Melvin. He was little, and he looked as if he got shoved around quite a bit, but he didn't give me a hard time about ordering the 7-Up. I waited fifteen minutes, then I called Jill Thaddeus back. She'd talked to Sterling. All systems were go.

The sliver of moon had been swallowed up by dark clouds, and there was a fine drizzle of rain, all the way back to the city. I still enjoyed the ride. There were plenty of things to think about.

Sheriff Bryce Canyon had been busted, too. The authorities had about a dozen counts against him. He'd do some long, hard time. With what I'd been able to add, thanks mostly to Crys—I mean Taffy—they'd busted Nails not only for conspiracy to distribute narcotics and for running the chop shop, but they'd also nailed him for murder one—two counts. Tank Thaddeus and old man Tucker.

Taffy had already wormed most of it out of them. Stinky and Nails had indeed killed old man Tucker. Sterling had paid them for the hits. Whether they'd turn state's evidence so that the feds could try Sterling too was another story. Taft was skeptical. There was that little matter of the prosecutor's being a member of Sterling's country club, and the problem of the politicians who'd probably been paid off. It was always a lot harder to bust someone of Sterling's ilk than it was to round up a litter of drug-crazed bikers—especially when, if Sterling was busted, *he* might talk, too! Taffy had also learned that Nails and Stinky had killed Tank Thaddeus. Sterling had told them to do it in my office so that I'd get off his case, so that I'd have a few nightmares.

Sterling! That bastard!

Maybe if I could just grab him by the balls I could make him squeal loud enough to put himself away right alongside Nails and Stinky and Jonesie and Snake—and all the others who specialized in destroying other people. Maybe. Anyway, I was sure as hell going to try.

Taffy had indeed known that Nails and Stinky killed old man Tucker and dumped his body in the irrigation ditch. Sterling had just given the order the day before. Uriah Tucker had been making too many demands, once he'd learned what was going on. He'd started to talk too much. Taffy had sent me to the irrigation ditch on purpose. She'd known how close-knit the little biker family was to the sheriff, had known that all the evidence was soon to vanish. Canyon was not only the judge and jury in Desolado; he'd also been the coroner and county recorder. And sweet Taffy had also been responsible for keeping Taft and Tafoya informed of my movements in the region. She'd let them know every time I'd dropped by.

What the hell, they'd had the motel phone bugged, too, along with several others. That was how they'd known I'd called about my rental car, why they'd shown up when they did, to work me over.

Yeah, that's right, I hadn't forgotten about that. But, under the circumstances, what the hell. That was already ancient history.

The city lights were on the horizon, lying beneath the tatters of the last few rainclouds. All of a sudden I felt good. I pushed a random tape into my tape deck and hit the ON button. Right in the middle of "Whistle While You Work."

CHAPTER
THIRTY-FIVE

I'D HAD JILL TELL STERLING THAT THE LOBBY DOOR OF my office building would be unlocked.

I left my office door unlocked, too.

I stepped through the darkness and pulled my drapes open, letting a faint light into the room. The luminous dial on my watch said eleven forty-five. I'd made some good time driving back to the city. I sat down at my desk and swiveled my chair around so that I could see out the window.

Four stories below me, a rusty oil tanker and two barges lay at berth, their lights glistening against the black waters of the harbor. The Super Sam cargo cranes were at rest, too, their prehensile skeletons towering up almost as high as my window, and black as the charred bones of a fire-inundated reptile in some far distant time.

Behind them, across the bay, shimmering reflections of light spilled out across the top of the blue-black waters. In a mirror image, the roller coaster rose above the bay—a serpentine of glitter against the diaphanous blackness of the sky.

The midway and various rides made spinning, swinging, rotating necklaces and pendants of light, mostly a yellow-white shimmer splashed through with sparks and spangles of red, blue, green. . . .

I could easily pick out the slowly spinning Ferris wheel from the gaudy resplendence. Once in a while a faraway shout or a fragment of music drifted across the water. It was summer in a land where it was perpetual summer. The amusement park wouldn't close until two A.M.

There was a little rap on my office door. I glanced at my watch. Twelve-oh-one.

I stood up, smoothed my pants, then turned on the desk lamp. I stepped over to the door, pulled it open. "What's up, Doc?" I asked.

Dr. Worthington Sterling's face was taut with a mixture of exasperation and indignation. He tried to smile, but the effort was fruitless. "Good evening, Mr. Weatherby. I was told that you have something that belongs to me?"

"Come on in and sit down, Doc." I returned to my swivel chair, gesturing him to the brown leather armchair across from me. He stayed by the door.

His skin looked pasty in this light. Nostrils flaring slightly, he said, "I considered calling the police. But when my fiancée gave me your message, I decided I'd give you a chance to explain your peculiar behavior."

I hit the little button beneath my desk that activates the tape recorder. "I guess you must be referring to your files."

He moved to the chair and stood beside it. "I am a professional man. Those files contain privileged information about my clients. Aside from breaking into my office, what you've done is highly illegal. If you'd be so kind as to return them, I believe we could forget this unpleasant incident. I realize that people of your stripe believe that they have special privileges."

"I want a kilo of coke." I felt like playing with him.

"I beg your pardon?" He'd drawn himself up to full height as he talked, trying to intimidate me.

I rolled my chair back a few inches and swung my loafers up onto my desk. "You might as well sit down, Doc. This might take a while."

He sat. Cautiously. On the edge of the chair. But he sat.

"It's simple, really," I continued. "I'll trade you your files for a kilo of coke."

The old nostrils flared again. "If this isn't the most ridiculous, repugnant—"

"Can it, Doc. If you want your files back, get me the coke."

His face was turning to the color of dark putty. "This is blackmail," he said.

"Extortion," I corrected him.

"What makes you think I want those files badly enough to go to the trouble of buying cocaine for you?" Why do you want it, anyway? Are you an addict?"

I shook my head. "I know you want those files because you're here. And because *I* know why you had them in the first place."

The sides of his lips curled under and his slender hands balled into fists. "You are an insolent—"

I wagged my finger at him. "Now, now, sticks and stones. See that gray throw rug beside your chair? Slide it over a bit."

"What? Have you gone daft?"

I stood up, walked around the desk, and slid the rug aside with my foot, exposing a wide, dark stain on the hardwood floor. "See that?" I asked.

Perplexed, he said, "A stain on the floor. I don't see what that has to do with—"

"That's Tank Thaddeus's blood. I had to rearrange my furniture and buy that throw rug to cover the stains. Sometimes I can still smell the blood." I stepped back and sat on the edge of my desk, folding my arms. Now I was looking down at him. The silver hair was thinning on the crown of his head. He had that little up-and-down frown on his face. Haughty. I said, "You know something? Every time I see that gray throw rug, I think of what Tank Thaddeus looked like the night I found his body. And every time I think of that, I think of Nails McNulty. And every time I think of Nails McNulty, I think of you."

He didn't like that progression. His face had gone sullen

and mean, and his hand was fidgeting around with something he carried in pocket. But he was listening, almost fascinated.

"They busted Nails," I said.

"Wha—?"

"Tonight. Out in Desolado. The feds got the whole greasy bunch. They'll talk. You know that. And with these files, I can back up everything they say about your part in the murders of Uriah Tucker and Tank Thaddeus."

He sprang to his feet. "You lying bastard!"

I picked up the telephone and offered it to him. "Call the motel."

A .22 Derringer materialized in his hand. He aimed it at me and twisted out the words: "I—want—those—files. Now!"

"So impatient," I said. I wasn't especially worried. My jacket was comfortably unbuttoned and my .38 was just inside it.

Rage passed over his face, and for just a second he almost pulled the trigger. Then reason returned. He jerked the gun, trying to lift me up with it as if he had me on an invisible hook connected to it. "Get those files!"

"So you admit the files are important?"

"I admit nothing."

"Are you going to kill me?"

"That depends on you."

"How so?"

"Get me those flies, you third-rate shamus!"

I folded my arms, keeping my hand close to the butt of my gun. "I'm just curious. I want to know why you killed them."

His face was twisted into lines of contempt, his nose and mouth pinched up. "Because they were just like you, shamus. They didn't know when to step back and shut up. They kept getting in my way. Like you've been doing. *Where are those files*?" He ground his teeth in his frustration. His knuckles were white.

I underestimated him. I had what I needed on him now,

and I felt too good about it. I started to slip my hand casually into my jacket to pull out the .38, saying as I moved, "If you can find them, you can have—"

His gun made a flat, spitting sound. Fire licked at my shoulder and spun me partway around.

I caught myself. Then I was up, coming in at him with my .38 in my hand as he sprinted for the door. He darted to one side and his second and last shot slammed past me. Then he scrambled through the door, dashing down the hall, down the exit stairway.

I got off a shot, but I missed him.

But I was right behind him. I was going to step on him like a cockroach, mash him, cream him, smash that simpering, cruel face into blood pudding. If I could catch him!

He ran fast. But I was going to get him. I was going to punch his headlights out! I ignored the pain in my shoulder and ran.

We clumped down the stairway, taking three, four steps at a time. He crashed through the alley door. I was right behind him, almost had him—I dove at him in a flying tackle, but he'd darted behind a garbage can just as I moved and I grabbed a circle of corrugated metal instead of him. The can tipped over, spilling heaps of watermelon rinds, eggshells, coffee grounds, partly eaten hamburgers, and other gunk over me, covering the sidewalk around me. He was gone, dancing past the garbage, then streaking through the alley. I slid about two feet on a banana peel, caught my balance, then I was after him.

He was at the curb, sliding behind the wheel of his shiny new Mercedes. The engine purred to life.

I lunged at the rear bumper, trying to grab it, but he stomped on the gas. The car jerked away from me.

I bolted across the street, slid into my BMW, revved her up, did a quick bootlegger's U-turn, and, with a screech of tires, I was just behind him again.

A man crossing the street jumped out of the way as Sterling peeled down Quaker, then screeched a two-wheeled right onto El Agua. He shot across three lanes of traffic, the other cars swerving and careening around to miss him. I moved into the flow more carefully.

A Yellow Cab sideswiped him, driving him onto the shoulder of the road. He almost took the embankment, swerving back and forth, the rear end of the car fishtailing, but then he had control again and he was back on the pavement, back in the far lane, pushing the Mercedes up to a cool seventy-five, then eighty miles an hour. Horns blared.

I was right behind him, the lights of the waterfront a blurred stream on either side of me.

I couldn't read the green-and-white sign above the off ramp to our left, but I'd seen it, knew what it said: AIRPORT EXIT. Sterling was doing a kamikaze into the traffic again, trying to make the exit. I hit my brakes. A city bus was barreling down the road, toward the off ramp. The driver saw Sterling, hit his horn, swerved into the next lane, and hurled past the off ramp, just as Sterling jerked his own wheel to miss the bus. Sparks flew along the side of the bus where it scraped against the car, and then the rear end of the bus somehow grabbed Sterling's bumper. The Mercedes was behind the bus, being scooped along by it, the Mercedes half sideways, the bus driver jerking his steering wheel back and forth to try to dislodge the car before the momentum wrecked the bus.

The car's bumper ripped off. Three other cars, brakes screaming, tail-ended one another as Sterling turned his wheel and drove straight across the boulevard and skidded sideways, wrong way, into an off ramp. I slammed on my own brakes, did another bootlegger's turn, and I was on top of him again.

His car was smashed up bad. The bumper was gone, the rear end was scraping on the tires, the left side was smashed up, and the left rear fender was gone. But it was still running. Sterling turned his head and looked at me, giving me a silvery version of Oilcan Charlie's mustache twirl, and then he stomped on the gas again, skidding every which way.

The red, green, and gold glitter of an enormous sign

blazed up above and to the left: PACIFIC FUNWAY AMUSE-
MENT PARK. Sterling slammed on his brakes, skidded into
the parking lot in front of the massive stone gateway, and
tried to turn around. His wheels locked.

Sterling gunned the engine, trying to get the car moving
again. I skidded up behind him, turned off my ignition,
and jumped out.

He spun his head around, saw me walking toward him,
and flew out of the still-running car. He made straight for
the turnstile in the entryway of the monolithic stone wall—
the false front of the amusement park.

My breath was coming fast, more from anger than ex-
ertion. I moved along behind him, wondering if now was
the time to use my gun.

Too many people around. Unless I managed to stop him
with one shot, there was no telling what Sterling might do.

The kid manning the turnstile was about sixteen. It was
late; things had slowed down. He had stepped over to
chat with the cute little blonde who was selling tickets.

He'd just turned around when he saw Sterling flying at
him. He did a quick double take, darted first one way then
the other, then he fell flat on his face, yelling, "Hey! Watch
out!" Sterling sprinted up to the turnstile, leaped over it—
and I was still right behind him! The kid stood up right
after I'd jumped the gate, shouting, "Hey! Hey! Hey!"

The sounds of a calliope filled the air. The smells of
popcorn, cotton candy, and caramel apples hung in the sea
breeze. People jumped off the flagstone pathway as Sterling
crashed through. He ran across a little bridge over a non-
existent stream, and he darted back and forth across a miniature golf course, looking over his shoulder to see if I was
still behind him.

I was.

Screams and shouts came from every direction now, and
I couldn't tell for sure if it was because we were disturbing
the natural chaos of things or if the noises were coming
from the rides. The crosshatched wood of the roller coaster
was just behind us, the Ferris wheel just ahead; the midway
was off to our right.

Sterling glanced over his shoulder to see where I was again. A middle-aged woman with rock-gray hair, wearing a polka-dotted pantsuit, was just about to hit a ball through a little windmill and across a moat. She had her back to us, her butt stuck out, her knees bent. She concentrated on the ball, got the golf club just so. But Sterling turned around too late to keep from crashing straight into her. The impact sent her flying. He reeled sideways, caught his balance, turned, and ran straight through the windmill, blades collapsing around him, thin wood cracking and ripping. He caught his balance again and staggered into the moat, the woman screaming obscenities after him.

It must have been slippery in there. Maybe there was moss on the bottom of the moat, because he lost his footing, slipped in, and then he was up and out, on his feet like a cat, hurling himself forward again.

He trampled through a bed of violets, petunias, sweet peas, and lilacs. I trampled right behind him. He darted in and behind the thick lattice work of the roller coaster's base. I was right on his heels, almost had him once; but he spun, dodged, and got away.

He fled in and out of the darkness behind the boards, past the roller coaster, and into the chained-off area where the Octopus swooped up and down and spun around, its lights flashing. The mechanic who ran the thing yelled at us, "Get out of here, you idiots! You want to get killed?" We were past the Octopus, past the chain-link fence, and heading for the merry-go-round.

The calliope music wound down, then started up again, playing Strauss's Blue Danube Waltz through its huffing and puffing steam whistles. The carousel started to turn.

There were about a dozen people on the horses, mostly older kids and teenagers. Two punk rockers, about twelve or thirteen, sat on bright blue horses, their red, violet, and yellow epoxied hair standing a full foot above their heads and making them look like exotic birds, their fluorescent clothing only slightly phosphorescent in the lights around the top of the machine.

Sterling crashed past them, then leaped into the pit in

the middle, where a grizzled old man was operating the
levers that kept the machine and the music going. He leaned
into a lever as Sterling ran past him, and the Blue Danube
degenerated into the coughing and wheezing and sputtering
of an asthmatic woodwind section.

Sterling paused, stepped backward, and tumbled into
the long lever that controlled the brake. The machine
stopped on a dime. People tumbled backward, fell off
their horses, screamed, yelled. The two punk rockers,
tumbling around beneath the two blue horses, grabbed
the wooden legs. "Hot ride! Hey! Chill out and let's do
it again!" they yelled.

Sterling was up, over the far side, and off the merry-go-
round. He raced under the glittering, spinning Ferris
wheel—the operator jumping out of the way, then shouting
after him. Then Sterling dashed up a little grassy slope and
ran beside a knee-high latticework wall that held a bumper
car ring inside. Man, that guy could run.

He looked around to see how close I was, lost his balance, and tumbled over the wall. He landed legs sticking
up, inside a shiny red bumper car. Someone bumped into
it, and it spun away.

I jumped the wall, tried to catch him, but the cars, half
of them holding people, were spinning every which way.
People crashed into one another and spun off while the
operator poured on the juice. A loudspeaker blared some
acid rock, music to maim your mother by.

I was standing in the ring. Two cars whizzed past, barely
missing me. People yelled. I could see Sterling, clear on
the other side of the ring now, up against the cushion,
trying to get up and out of the car. Someone rammed him.
He lost his balance and went spinning away. A fat woman
whizzed up. She almost hit me. She screamed, then spun
her wheel just in time to keep from knocking my legs out
from under me. She hit the cushion instead. The car looked
like a cup around her bottom half, and she had a lot of
momentum from all that weight. She went sailing backward. A chubby, freckle-faced ten-year-old with brick-red
hair appeared to be with her. He grinned widely as he

sailed past me, steered his purple car around until he had some momentum of his own, then crashed his car into hers as it came sailing backward. At the impact, they both screamed.

I leaped out of the way as two punk rockers zoomed past me, spun around, then whizzed past me again. The girl had her head completely shaved except for a three-foot-high epoxied purple-and-lavender crest that stuck straight up from the middle of her head. The boy, about the same age, had long hair that stuck straight up in spikes. It had been dyed a bright canary yellow. His eyes were narrowed from the intensity of crashing into the girl. The second time he nailed her, she screamed, spun around a few times, then started snapping her fingers in rhythm to the deafening music as her car spun away. The boy started crashing randomly into anyone who got close.

Sterling had managed to get his legs into the car so that he could step on the pedals, turn the wheel. He had some control now. I saw him whiz past me, glaring at me.

Suddenly the fat lady was back, wheeling toward me, screaming "Wheeeee," as I jumped out of the way just in time to avoid being crushed between her green car and the purple car her kid was in.

Sterling's silver hair bobbed up above all the other heads at the far side of the ring. He was scrambling up, about to climb out of the car. I was by the front gate now. I grabbed the attendant by the collar and shouted, "Stop! Stop the cars!"

He seemed to go into shock. "Whatever you say, buddy, whatever you say—" I then realized that I was still holding my .38.

He leaned on a lever, and suddenly the cars were all crashing into one another, flying by, spinning around, rushing at one another as if the whole world had been spun into fast motion. "Damn!" the attendant yelled. "Turned it the wrong way!" He leaned on the lever, trying to reverse it. Nothing happened. "Son of a gun,"

he said, shaking his head, yanking at the lever. "Stuck!"
He kept pulling.

Sterling had tumbled back into his shiny red car, and it
seemed to have taken on a life of its own as all the other
cars crashed into it, bounced back, then crashed again from
a different angle. The fat lady had her hands up over her
head, not even trying to steer. She was screaming. Her kid
had a grin like a slice of watermelon on his face. He was
crashing his car into hers over and over again, fast-framing
it, hell-bent-for-leather, laughing and yelling, and then
doing it again. The two punk rockers spun around and
crashed into everyone and everything in sight. They had
identical expressions of ecstasy on their faces. From the
loudspeaker, the beat went on.

An empty blue car came spinning by. I jumped into it
and took off after Sterling, who was spinning around,
crashing into the fat lady—then he was being bounced back
and forth, back and forth, between the fat lady and the kid.
His eyes widened as he saw me coming, but he couldn't
seem to get away from between them.

The attendant was frantic. "Help! Help! Security! This
damned machine's stuck. These people are going nuts!
Heeellllp!"

I bounced off the railing, bounced off a girl's car, and
then came dead in on Sterling in his little red car. He
fished into his shirt pocket and brought out something. It
was the Derringer! Somehow he'd found the time to re-
load!

I still had my .38 in my hand. Deftly, I steered the
bumper car with my left hand, drew a bead on Sterling
with my right—as much as I could, considering the motion
of my car and the motion of his. I had him sighted—he
was drawing a bead on me, too—when the fat lady came
crashing into me, an expression of pure horror on her face.
She screamed, "Oh, heavens, he-eeeelp!" She sent me
spinning before she crashed into the railing, then bounced
back toward Sterling's car.

He was halfway standing, paying no attention to anyone
or anything but me. His car was moving along slowly for

a change, but the lady's car was coming toward him. He saw her coming, jumped out of his car, spread his legs like a sharpshooter, and aimed that gun. My car was stuck in place, spinning around in circles, the motion interfering with my own aim. I couldn't get it stopped so I could get out, couldn't do anything—

But I *could* see that Sterling's finger was clenching on the trigger, that the car he'd been in was sailing away, shoved by the fat lady's car. Now Sterling could see that he had me. I spun back around, saw him standing there, relishing the moment, his cold blue eyes staring straight into mine every time I spun around, promising me a cold, dark grave. I spun again. And again. He was still there, ready.

But wait!

The fat lady's car had swung back around, was moving toward me, was gaining momentum. I held my breath, spun again, and tried to get my bearings so I could aim my .38.

Her car was coming straight at Sterling from behind. He paid no attention to it as he relished what he was about to do to me. I breathed a silent prayer.

My car stopped spinning just as her car crashed into him from behind. It threw him to one side, and the two punk rockers' cars were bearing down on him now as he scrambled across the concrete floor, scurrying after the gun, which had flown from his hand as he fell.

But the fat lady was on the rebound; her kid was spinning in. . . . Sterling was pinned in, had no place to run to. He looked around. His gun was forgotten for the moment as, with a growing panic, he realized what was happening. Cars coming from all four directions, coming faster, closer—he jerked his head around again, looking for an escape. Then he looked upward. With a little leap, he grabbed on to a fat black cable that hung from the electrical wiring that webbed through the rafters of the wooden cupola of the roof.

"No! Don't touch—" The attendant screamed just as a hideous zap of electricity shot from the black cable and through Sterling. Sparks flew through and off him as he jerked, relaxed, jerked again. He looked like a cartoon cat that's just stuck its finger into a light socket.

But the cable was live, and Sterling couldn't let go. He jerked yet again. Sparks flew.

The lights in the bumper car rink blazed, dimmed, blazed, dimmed again, synchronized to Sterling's *danse macabre*.

The lights went out. The loudspeakers died. Except for the cries and moans of the others in the bumper cars, the rink was suddenly quiet, illumined now only by the light that washed in from the other rides. The few cars that were still in motion were coming to a stop.

Dr. Worthington Sterling had at last let go of the cable—or had it let go of him? He lay in a lifeless heap in the middle of the bumper car rink, the burnt-out cable swinging back and forth above him, the smell of burned wiring and rubber and the smell of charred flesh strong in the air. The bumper cars had all fanned out around him. The attendant was yelling, "It ain't my fault. I told them to get that frigging thing fixed—" while the girl with the lavender-purple hair kept repeating, "Gross, man. Gag me with a spoon. Positively *awesome!*" The fat lady said, "Whoosh," as she climbed out of her car in the same way that she'd have peeled off a girdle. The little boy, still in his car, whined, "Aw, Ma, do we have to quit so soon?"

I stood, stunned, looking at the crumpled, charred body of Dr. Feelgood. Ashes to ashes. But I felt no sense of victory, no sense of conquest. Even in death Dr. Worthington Sterling had managed to alter the world. The evil Pygmalion had turned it into something colorless, lifeless, and artificial.

The attendant was staring at my shirt. I put my hand to my shoulder, felt something wet, and pulled it away. Blood. The side of my shirt was sopped through with blood from where Sterling's bullet had creased my flesh. But even the wound was numbed.

I gave the attendant my phone number, told him to call the cops and then have them get in touch with me.

Then I walked back out through the turnstile to my car.

CHAPTER
THIRTY-SIX

IN LESS THAN AN HOUR THE COPS WERE AT MY DOOR. I talked to them for about another hour, gave them the key to my office, told them to go down and get the tape recording I'd made of Sterling's unwitting confession. All the while they were there, my shoulder throbbed and ached. When they left, I decided to see a doctor—a real one.

I got dressed and drove to the hospital, sat there for three hours waiting for someone to look at me. At last a doctor examined my shoulder. Just a flesh wound, but a good flesh wound. No serious damage, but I'd lost enough blood to keep old man Thaddeus happy for a month. The doctor wanted to keep me in the hospital. I wanted to go home. I went.

It was a lousy morning. The dank night sky had dissolved into a gray mist, then into a fine drizzle. As I turned up Sherwood Road and toward the canyon, the rain gusted in, deluging the car, the road—I turned on my headlights.

Home again, home again.

I undressed. I wanted a shower but couldn't take one because of the bandages. I mopped myself up as best I could, then lay down to sleep, perchance *not* to dream. . . .

My phone rang.

I argued with myself about answering it, then decided

that maybe it was the cops again with more questions. Better to answer the phone than have them come back over. I picked up the receiver. "Weatherby here."

"Good morning, Sunshine."

I was grouchy, tired; I'd lost a lot of blood. The rain outside was permeating my world with gloom. I growled, "Who in hell is this, anyway?"

"You've already forgotten me? After you saved my life?"

"Crys—I mean, Taffy?"

"Well, at least you remember me. For a minute there I wondered."

"Sorry if I'm a little grouchy. I just got back from the hospital. I got shot last night."

"It finally happened, huh?" Not a trace of sympathy there. Then she said, "I already heard. You nailed Sterling."

"Something like that."

'I'm going to come over. I'll bring a magnum of champagne so we can celebrate. I had a pretty good night, too, you know."

I groaned. "Couldn't you bring me a pint of blood instead?"

"Whatever you want. Whatever it is, I'm going to come over and play nurse. I was up all night, too, doing some of the wrap-up on Operation Snow White. I could use a day's rest. Want me to bring you anything?"

"Just yourself. On the double. My address is—"

"I know. I'm a fed, remember? I can find out anything. I'll be there in under an hour. 'Bye."

I sat up and blinked my eyes. Just like that the sun was shining, even though the rain still pattered down on my roof.

ABOUT THE AUTHOR

JANICE M. TUBBS-MILLER is a longtime resident of Honolulu, a perfect place for a crime buff. Her formal education is an eclectic montage of psychology, sociology, criminology, literature (English, French, and Russian), and all forms of academic intrigue. She considers herself a generalist with a perverse obsession for sleuthing—which has led her deep into the inner workings of the heroin traffic, in and out of the various affairs of several policing agencies, and in and out of a lot of trouble.

Weatherby is Ms. Miller's crime fiction debut.

Attention Mystery and Suspense Fans

Do you want to complete your collection of mystery and suspense stories by some of your favorite authors? John D. MacDonald, Helen MacInnes, Dick Francis, Amanda Cross, Ruth Rendell, Alistar MacLean, Erle Stanley Gardner, Cornell Woolrich, among many others, are included in Ballantine/Fawcett's new Mystery Brochure.

For your FREE Mystery Brochure, fill in the coupon below and mail it to:

12